"You will come with his eyes shimmering with the absolute confidence she would. That she'd go with him. Bend to his will and let him take charge.

"I will help you remember, Emma," he promised.

"What if I don't *want* to remember you?" she asked, because someone—something—was lying to her, and if it wasn't him... It wasn't her body. It was her mind, wasn't it? And the mind did things to protect the body. The soul. The *heart*.

"What if my mind has blanked you out on purpose?" she asked. "To protect me from you?"

"I am no threat to you, Emma," he said roughly. "We are married. I am your husband. Your protector. Trust me to protect you now."

Marriage. Husband. Protector.

Those words did something inside her. Something she didn't want to recognize.

But she couldn't deny the temptation of it.

Lela May Wight grew up with seven brothers and sisters. Yes, it was noisy, and she often found escape in romance books. She still does, but now she gets to write them, too! She hopes to offer readers the same escapism when the world is a little too loud. Lela May lives in the UK with her two sons and her very own hero, who never complains about her book addiction—he buys her more books! Check out what she's up to at lelamaywight.com.

Books by Lela May Wight

Harlequin Presents

His Desert Bride by Demand
Bound by a Sicilian Secret
The King She Shouldn't Crave

Visit the Author Profile page
at Harlequin.com.

ITALIAN WIFE WANTED

LELA MAY WIGHT

Harlequin

PRESENTS

Harlequin® PRESENTS™

Recycling programs for this product may not exist in your area.

ISBN-13: 978-1-335-93944-9

Italian Wife Wanted

Copyright © 2024 by Lela May Wight

 Harlequin Enterprises ULC
22 Adelaide St. West, 41st Floor
Toronto, Ontario M5H 4E3, Canada
www.Harlequin.com

Printed in Lithuania

MIX
Paper | Supporting responsible forestry
FSC® C021394

ITALIAN WIFE WANTED

Emma and Dante's love story is dedicated to *all* the Birmingham princesses.

The Brummy princess in the high-rise tower with your black, curly hair, the princess in the first-floor maisonette, or the second floor with no hair at all, the princess in the house with too-thin walls...

One day, your prince will come.

CHAPTER ONE

THE CAR MOVED smoothly down the road. A road that wouldn't dare to have any imperfections. No potholes. No uneven surfaces to jar the elite residents it welcomed home.

And Emma Cappetta was coming home.

She was one of the elite in her chauffeur-driven car. In her designer black skirt suit and red-soled heels with metal tips that clattered on hard floors and sank deeply into newly turned soil.

The car stopped, and Emma stepped out into the night.

Her feet ached, her body hurt and her heart was wounded.

She paused at the bottom of the white stone steps. Her hand resting on the black metal handrail, she stared at the black door and gold knocker, at the entrance to the five-storey Edwardian building she'd called home for almost a year.

She'd only been away for fourteen days, enough to pack up her mother's life and prepare for today, her mother's funeral.

But oh, how easily she'd slipped back into her

old life in Birmingham, how easily it had welcomed her back, how comfortable she'd felt in the child-hood home she'd shared with her mum. The photos of them on the walls. The warmth. The smell. She'd slept so soundly in her old bed with the neighbour's conversation drifting clearly through the thin walls.

The estate, the crumbling roads, the potholes, the chatter of children out too late playing in the com-munity playground…it had embraced her as if she'd never left.

Two weeks. That's all it had taken. Two weeks to unmask the lie of the life she'd been living for al-most a year. She didn't belong here in London, in this beautiful house.

This wasn't…*home*.

The door opened and she moved through it, her throat tightening as she did.

She took the first step, and another, until she stood face-to-face with the dipped head of the butler.

'Mrs Cappetta,' he acknowledged. 'Would you like some tea to be arranged for you in the sitting room?'

Emma smiled, but it was barely a twitch. 'No, thank you, James.' She moved past him, her heels clicking on the marble-floored reception area.

'Is there anything else I can get for you?'

Dante?

Her nose pinched.

She still wanted him.

And that want was like a constant hunger in her stomach. Inside her. Even now, when the veil had lifted from her eyes and she knew the undeniable truth: that she meant nothing to her husband.

She was a fool.

Today had been her mother's funeral, and he hadn't come. Hadn't called. Hadn't sent a card.

The one time she'd *really* needed him, he'd hadn't been there.

Just like your dad.

Emma's heart clenched.

What had she expected? Her husband was only ever there for the thrill. For the sex. For her body. Never for anything…*real*.

'No, I don't need anything,' she told James, because she had no physical needs. What she had needed was her husband's support. His presence. His compassion.

And it wasn't just that he hadn't been there; it was the very fact she needed him at all. That realisation was unravelling everything she'd ever believed about herself, about their relationship. And about this life she'd been living with Dante.

Her heart ached acutely behind her breastbone.

'If there's nothing else, Mrs Cappetta…'

'Thank you.'

James nodded and left her alone.

Alone as she'd been all day.

Just today?

The voice in her head mocked her. Because it was true. It had taken the death of her mother, her funeral, for her to understand.

But now she did understand.

The weight on her shoulders doubled, anchoring her to the spot.

Her eyes moved, taking in the plush silk rugs, the hand-carved and intricate side tables with professional lighting installed to highlight the priceless art hanging in just the right spot to awe and please.

It was a museum of priceless artefacts collected and displayed in a house that showed no signs—no evidence—of the people it housed.

No evidence of *them*.

It was further proof she didn't belong here.

The inner-city girl who had grown up surrounded by discoloured high-rises had no business here in Mayfair.

She had no right—no claim—to any of it.

The tendons contracted in her throat.

She hadn't realised it before, hadn't seen it, but she was in too deep.

Had she already fallen victim in the same way her mother had? Fallen in—

No. This wasn't love.

Love didn't exist. It was an illusion. And her mother had been punished for her folly. She'd been left broken-hearted time and time again. It's what had killed her, led to a heart attack at forty-three.

Emma straightened her spine.

The lie of love had killed her mother.

And it would kill her too if she allowed these feelings to take hold of her.

Emma slipped off her shoes where she stood and

made her way to the spiral staircase. Two at a time, she climbed them.

She entered her bedroom. *Their* bedroom.

At the sight of the perfectly made bed, heat engulfed her. She couldn't help thinking of the nights, the mornings or the afternoons she'd spent in it. In his arms.

Sex wasn't the problem. It never had been. In fact, it's what had started it all.

Emma couldn't let herself think of that now.

She moved to the desk positioned by the balcony doors to the view of the secret garden below.

There were only three secret gardens in London. Emma and Dante had visited all of them before they settled on this one. On this view from their bedroom. On this house.

He'd never promised her a home. He'd promised her a year. One year to allow the chemistry that raged between them to burn itself out.

And she hadn't been able to say no.

She'd agreed to the terms of this marriage because she'd wanted what her mother had never had. *Security.* Financially and emotionally.

When had it changed? she wondered. When had she started to want...*more*? More of Dante's time? His friendship? Companionship? Support?

Because she wanted all those things, didn't she? Had needed them today and felt their absence when he hadn't been at her side.

She couldn't really be mad; she hadn't directly

asked him to be there. But she'd told him the day and the time of the funeral service.

Emma wanted to wail as the truth assaulted her.

When had she got in so deep that his absence hurt?

She twisted the gold band on her finger.

It meant nothing. It was nothing more than a certificate of purchase. A twelve-month rental plan that she'd willingly agreed to.

And she hated it. Hated herself for how attached she'd become to a man.

For nearly twelve months, she'd waited for him, been ready for him. For him to visit her bed. A bed they shared when he returned from his endless business trips abroad that he'd never taken her, his wife, on. And those trips had got longer. And longer.

Marriage was the lie she'd always believed it was, wasn't it?

Her relationship with Dante was no different from the relationship her parents shared. A relationship where her mother was always waiting for her father to come back to her.

Emma believed she'd created something different. That she'd been in control in a way her mother never had been.

She sighed. *Heavily.*

She was still lying to herself, wasn't she?

It wasn't the marriage that was the lie. The marriage was everything Dante had promised it would be.

She'd changed. She wanted more. More than

she knew Dante could ever give. And knowing that would kill her.

Emma padded back across the room and threw open her walk-in wardrobe. So many clothes. So many gifts he'd given her. So many *things*.

And he could keep them all.

These things meant nothing, not to her, not to him.

Even she was a possession he kept shiny and clean, in preparation for the time he'd take her out of her box and display her for his pleasure.

She was only an extension of his collection.

She wasn't part of the elite. This wasn't her home, and what she'd agreed to wasn't a marriage.

Not the marriage *she* needed anyway.

Not anymore.

She opened the drawers and withdrew every velvet box and bag, lined them up on the bed in an array of colours and sizes. Over two dozen gifts he'd presented her with every time he returned to her, right before he'd seduced her. Bedded her. And then left. Over and over again.

She gazed at her left hand, at her engagement ring, the blue stone in its centre. Her birthstone. Then her gaze moved to the plain gold band. Her wedding ring.

They meant nothing. More meaningless gifts.

But the urge was to keep them. To leave them there, to remind herself what happened when you let yourself *feel*.

No.

She slipped the rings off and placed them in the middle of the pile of gifts.

Would he even recognise the symbolic importance of her rings there with all the other jewels?

She pulled out a single piece of paper and an envelope from her side drawer.

What to write?

She was angry at him, but at herself most of all. Angry for wanting things she'd decided long ago that she couldn't have if she was to keep her heart safe.

How did she explain this wasn't about love, that it wasn't him that had broken his promise? It was *her*.

She picked up the fancy ink pen and wrote three words he'd understand. Three words that would have given him the permission to end their marriage.

She collected her rings, and dropped them inside the envelope, with her note, and sealed it.

She placed it on her pillow.

When he returned, *this* would be the first place he'd come. To find her willing and waiting. As she always had been.

Except this time she wouldn't be here.

Emma turned and made her way out of the room and down the stairs. She slipped her heels back on, walked to the front door and opened it. She stepped outside and gripped the handle to the door. She held on tight, looking back at the lie of the life she thought she could have had.

'Goodbye,' she said to the house, to the *things* and to him.

Emma pulled the door closed and let go of the handle. She let go of all the lies she'd told herself for the last year, and readied herself to face the bold truth of what came next.

Divorce.

Two days later...

Dante Cappetta signed his name with elegant flicks.

It was a simple document. It outlined as much as the first contract he'd presented to her. The only difference was the time they'd remain married.

Dante stared at the empty signature box. He didn't imagine it would be empty for long. Soon, so very soon, his wife would sign her name without hesitation and bind herself to him for an additional three years of marital bliss.

Four weeks remained on their original marriage contract, but there was no need to wait until then to present her with a new agreement.

He was...*satisfied.* And he wanted her to have this gift. An early present for being...*perfect.*

He closed the contract.

But he felt it. An easiness. Something close, he supposed, to contentedness, because the urge was not for *more* as it always was with the Cappetta men to climb higher peaks, or to parachute over more perilous terrains.

The urge was simply to keep things with Emma the same. To keep her.

He settled into the leather recliner and watched the lights twinkle over the dark city of London.

The Cappetta Travel Empire had its fingers in

every pie: airlines, boats, hotels. They had headquarters in every important travel capital, with offices everywhere else they were required, but never had one city taken precedence over another.

Dante simply went where he was most in demand, and before Emma, women chased *him*. Followed him to any God-given destination, and did all they could to attract his attention.

He'd eventually made a game of which socialite it would be *this* week. Sometimes they'd tried to seduce him in duos.

But never had he travelled for a woman. Never had he returned to any specific destination because his skin ached to feel a woman's touch. Never had he tried to beat the sun to make sure he was in a woman's bed before she woke to wake her with *his* kiss.

But he did these things for her.

For his wife.

Their marriage was a contract; it was not about love or friendship. It was a way of controlling the fire that raged between them. A way for him to have the one woman who consumed him, again and again, whenever he wanted.

He had thought one year would be enough. Enough to satisfy the hunger.

In the past, Dante had played by the rules his father had written. That playbook had suited him just fine. Until Emma… So many rules didn't apply to her because she was different from any other woman he'd ever taken to bed.

And that's why he was proposing they extend their

contract by an additional three. Because the heat between them was too hot to ignore. But most of all, because Emma understood the rules of their marriage and she played by them so beautifully. They wanted the same things.

The plane landed without ceremony.

Dante collected the contract, slipped it inside his briefcase and closed the golden clasps.

He descended the stairs and got into the waiting car.

Ten minutes and he'd be back at the house they shared.

He wasn't so naive. This obsession with her, his little crush, would end. *Eventually.* Then and only then would he end it.

But not yet.

Three more years should suffice. He was sure. And then he and she would part ways amicably.

He hadn't spoken to Emma for two weeks. But his people had informed him his wife had returned safely to their Mayfair residence two days ago.

Funerals, they were horrid things. When his father died, Dante had jumped out of a plane rather than attend. And what would have been the point anyway? Burying an empty casket seemed pointless. When people went missing at sea, there were no bodies.

Besides, funerals were for the living to mourn and weep, and to claim closure. None of which Dante required. He'd never loved his father. Never had a relationship with him that required closure. The only thing his father had left him was his playbook, the only inheritance Dante had ever required.

And Dante knew by heart the script his father had written: *never give away your power. Always be in control. Let no one get too close. Never let them leave first. Never give them the opportunity to hurt you.*

The only woman who had ever done that was his mother.

Technically, she'd left them both. Her husband and her son. But it mattered little. He'd couldn't remember her. He certainly didn't need her.

But Emma wasn't like him. And she had done all the dutiful things she thought a daughter should do for her mother's funeral. She had wanted closure. She hadn't felt the need to run from her past by whatever means necessary.

It was why he had never taken her with him when he was away on business. His work took him deep into dangerous territory, exploring unmapped lands and canyons. Emma didn't want to explore the unknown. She liked the status quo. *Normality.* And that's what he gave her.

That's why they worked so well.

He lived his life, and she lived hers, and then they both came back to each other. No mind games.

If she had a need, he met it. As he had for the entirety of their marriage—as he would continue to do until their marriage ended.

Their arrangement suited them both. And she was content. He knew, because why wouldn't she be happy? His billions give her access to everything she could ever want, including him.

The car travelled through London's sleeping streets until it reached the house he and Emma shared. Swiftly, he made his way inside, depositing his briefcase at the foot of the staircase.

Anticipation shot through him.

For twenty-one days he hadn't touched his wife, hadn't felt the warmth of her skin.

He'd flown through the night to reach her before the sun rose. Before the staff woke. Before *she* woke.

He eyed the curling stairs, with intricate carved patterns adorning the white banister. He knew which step creaked and which whined, which could alert her to his presence. They were the final part of his journey back to her.

His body pulsed.

The slow ascent was agonising. But finding his wife soft and pliant would be worth it.

Bed soft, he liked to call it, when the body was torn between waking and dreams. Everything, every muscle, oversensitised. And she'd come awake, alive with him beside her. Touching her.

He toed off his shoes, shrugged off his suit jacket and let it fall to the floor. He removed his tie. Attacked the buttons of his crisp, white shirt with silent precision, letting it float the way of his suit jacket.

The thrill remained the same as ever. The excitement of making love to her ever present.

It moved inside him now, as strong as the night they'd met.

Need.

He unbuckled his belt and guided his trousers and boxers down his firm thighs.

Oh, God, he was hard. *So hard.*

Naked now, he ascended the stairs with stealthy speed.

Adrenaline pumped through him. He almost growled at the ferocity of the anticipation of surprising her with his unexpected homecoming. But he remained silent.

He wanted to wake her with a kiss. A kiss she'd reciprocate with a speed that always floored him. Excited him beyond measure. Her effortless enthusiasm. Her absolute adoration of him.

Slowly, oh, so slowly, he opened the bedroom door.

Darkness.

He moved towards the bed on silent feet. He couldn't see a thing, but he knew this bedroom. This bed. His wife. Waiting for him. Curled into herself. Her blond hair would be strewn across the pillow, waiting for his fingers to grip it. He would draw her mouth to his.

He slipped between the sheets, reached for her. 'Emma?' he said, calling to her in the darkness. And he could taste it. The longing in every syllable of her name. The yearning to be in her arms and accept her welcome.

Her side of the bed was...*cold*.

It was a large bed. He moved closer. Stretched out his arms, his long legs, his feet—searching for her. The warmth of her tiny toes to stroke against his. Her soft body to pull into his.

Something on the bed—on her side—clattered to the floor.

He slammed on the lights.

Jewellery boxes. A dozen had toppled onto the floor. He picked up the only black velvet bag to remain on the bed, opened it and withdrew a necklace from within. It dangled between his fingers. A white gold chain tipped with the clearest diamond…

Where was she? It was barely four in the morning.

He dropped the necklace and bag onto the bed.

He pulled back the sheets and stepped out of the bed. His toes sunk into the carpet with every footfall as he opened her walk-in wardrobe. Nothing was out of place. Had she laid out all her jewellery to decide what to wear and forgotten to put them away? Had she gone out last night and had yet to return?

He frowned. Irritation crawled over his skin. Where would she have gone? With whom?

He didn't keep tabs on his wife, and he didn't give her a timetable of his whereabouts either. He didn't tell her if *this* work trip was any more dangerous than the last. His clients' needs differed.

He froze.

A white paper edge stuck up at a sharp triangular angle between the headboard and the pillow.

He freed it.

It was an envelope with his name on it.

Dante tore it open.

The contents fell onto the bed.

Her engagement ring.

Her wedding ring.

He stared at them.

She'd taken them off.

She'd never taken off her rings before. Not even in the shower. Neither had he. Not since she'd slipped it onto his finger in the courthouse.

And yet, here they were.

Her rings.

He turned the envelope upside down and shook it. A little rectangular slip of paper slipped free.

Her elegant handwriting swirled before his eyes: "I want out."

His body tightened with a pulse of emotion he didn't recognise. *Didn't like.*

But he felt stripped down. Exposed beyond his nakedness.

She'd left him?

No, she wouldn't leave him. Didn't have any reason to leave—

Realisation dawned.

He'd made a mistake. Miscalculated. By letting his wife know how much he wanted her, he'd given her everything she needed to play him like a fiddle.

She's never played games before.

No, she hadn't. But that didn't mean she wasn't playing games now. So, what did she want? More money? A larger settlement if she remained married to him?

His temples throbbed. It made no sense. It was completely out of character. And yet, she was gone. But that was what women did, wasn't it? They left when it suited them.

Dante picked up the simple gold band and slipped it onto his little finger. And there it sat beside his own.

He let out a deep, calming breath.

Emma would come back.

And when she did, he'd close the door in her face.

CHAPTER TWO

Three months later...

DANTE LOOKED DOWN at the rings on his fingers. He'd kept hers on, not for sentimental reasons, but as a reminder of how close he'd come to losing control. Letting his hunger for his wife become an obsession.

Determination straightened his spine.

He was indifferent to her now. But it was maddening how much of an effect her departure had had. How much he had allowed her to influence his life to begin with.

For three months, he hadn't accepted any jobs that would take him away from English waters. He hadn't been back to London either, but he'd remained close. Japan wasn't happy. Some of their most exclusive clients were demanding they have access to his personal expertise, wouldn't take no for an answer. People came to him, to his company, to provide them with the type of experiences they couldn't get anywhere else.

The Cappetta Travel Empire was built on his father's thrill-seeking adventures. His father had

revolutionised a small airline company into a rec-
ognisable brand. And Dante had inherited it all.

Being stuck on British soil was unwelcome. But
he couldn't leave, especially not now as he recalled
the doctor's words over the phone.

*Mr Cappetta, your wife has fallen. Bumped her
head. She's confused. She doesn't remember a lot
of things.*

His mother had claimed she'd fallen too. That was
how she'd found out she was pregnant. *A lie.* She'd
known all along, but the lie allowed her to manipulate his father. Manipulate his desire for an heir, an
heir he wanted little to do with raising but wanted
nonetheless. And his mother had got what she wanted
too: the means to live her life as she pleased, with the
money she got in exchange for her son.

Emma couldn't barter his flesh and blood. Dante
had made sure there would never be children in his
future.

You never thought you'd have a wife either.

After tonight, he wouldn't.

But the depth of Emma's deception was unexpected. And he hated he hadn't seen it coming. Over
the last three months, he'd talked himself in circles.
Doubt had riddled him.

She'd left everything behind, including a small
fortune in jewels. On the surface, it looked as though
she no longer wanted her things. No longer wanted…
him.

But he understood the truth.

His wife wanted something, because there was no

fathomable reason for her to leave, unless this was a play for power. *For more.*

And it was. He was sure of that.

Anyone's palms could be greased with the right lubrication.

'Sir,' the driver said. 'We're here.'

So they were. The drab inner-city hospital in Birmingham was so far away from the life he'd gifted to her. And the knowledge that she'd chosen to come back here speared him in the gut.

Emma's accent was rich. There had been no doubt of her origin when they'd met. But this city was nothing like the capital they'd lived in together. It was closer. The atmosphere was too intimate. The people were too much. Their melodic and soft accents somehow penetrated deeper.

Just like her? Is that why you haven't filed for divorce?

No, that was because Emma had plunged a knife into his solar plexus, and he knew the only way to drive out the blade was to see her again. To confirm that his sweet little wife was just like his mother, who had traded her unborn child for a fat cheque and a private island. Seeing Emma would confirm that she had been manipulating him all along.

He stepped out of the car, and night lights burned in a shimmering rainbow all around him. He looked over the nondescript concrete building with red letters lit up by a white background.

Accident and Emergency.

He moved towards it.

The electronic door slid open.

He eyed the A&E department. Stale and metallic, the air reeked. And it was...*cloying*. The reality of it. Humans littered the chairs and the floors. Zombified, they stared at a string of red letters floating across a screen, announcing an estimated wait time of six hours.

This would not have been the venue he would have expected for an attempt to woo him.

He felt a sense of powerlessness here. Hopelessness. That whatever happened in these walls was out of his control.

Did Emma understand that? Was that why she'd chosen this scenario? To toy with him? To make him feel powerless?

The two double doors to Dante's left opened, and two paramedics exited.

He moved through them, confident he'd find Emma somewhere in this rabbit warren.

The doctor who'd called had said an ambulance had brought Emma in and she was now waiting for the doctor to examine her, but A&E was busy. As her next of kin, he needed to arrive promptly as she was showing signs of distress. *Confusion*. She needed support.

He was sure the doctor's words had been calculated to trigger certain emotions in him. And delivered by a professional, they were all the more believable. Made it easier to alarm him, imagine how vulnerable she was. *Alone*.

He wasn't alarmed, but here he was.

The doors closed behind him.

Drawn curtains equalled full beds, didn't they? He'd never been in a hospital like this, but Dante understood. He'd read the papers. It was easy to see why Emma's doctor had been so easily persuaded to take part in her little ruse.

What if she isn't lying? She's never lied to you before. Never gone to these kinds of lengths to get your attention.

She *had* to be lying. He couldn't allow for any other scenario. He would call her out on her lies, she would sign the divorce papers and they'd be done once and for all.

His ears pricked as the low hum of conversations behind each makeshift cubicle peaked.

He moved. *Listening.*

'Thank you, Doctor.'

His neck snapped to the left as a white, cheap curtain was dragged back on a metal rail. A harried man with a tight smile nodded and withdrew from the cubicle.

And there she was.

Her blond fringe had grown and fell over her eyebrows. Thick silky strands framed her face, teasing at her high cheekbones before falling in a wave over her shoulders.

Oh, how he'd liked to play with her hair. Wrap it around his fist and draw her into his chest as her back pressed into him.

No, he wouldn't go there. He would not indulge in what had always been between them.

He focused himself and let his gaze travel down.
Her legs lay flat on top of sterile white starched
sheets as she sat up against an almost nonexistent
pillow. A white blouse covered her pert breasts and
a black pencil skirt hugged her hips and thighs.

The same little outfit she'd worn the night they'd
met.

As he brought his gaze back up her body to her
face, their gazes caught.

Wide, bright blue eyes met his. And he noted the
widening of her pupils.

'Doctor,' she acknowledged.

Was this her attempt at strengthening the ruse?

Slowly, he pulled the curtain back into place. 'No,'
he said, dismissing the idea of playing *that* game.
'I'm no doctor.'

'Then who are you?' Her pink lips parted, and his
mouth slickened. Unbidden. 'A nurse?' she pressed.
'A porter?'

'You really don't know who I am, Emma?' he
asked, and ignored the pressure building in his sternum. He knew she was faking, and yet… The conviction in her voice was impressive.

'Should I?' She shrugged. 'The doctor said lots of
things were going to happen. Someone would be with
me shortly to take me to a ward. And then something
about a psychiatrist and an MRI. Or some abbrevia-
tion of letters. But honestly, I feel fine.'

He moved closer and stood at the end of the bed.
'Of course you do.'

'I do,' she confirmed. 'I've already wasted so

many resources. I don't need to be in this bed taking it from someone who needs it.'

'You don't need it, Emma?' he asked, moving around the bed in purposeful strides. 'The bed? You don't require *my* assistance?' he baited. *Watched.* But she didn't flinch. Not a flicker of anything.

'I'm clumsy,' she said. 'It's untreatable, I'm afraid.'

'If you are untreatable,' he said, catching the lie as it was spoken, 'why come to a hospital for treatment?'

'The paramedic insisted.'

'Or *you* insisted?' he countered.

'*He* said he was following protocol.'

'And as the protocol would bring you here,' he said, watching her reaction, waiting for the penny to drop that he understood what she was doing, 'you thought you'd use it to your advantage?'

'My advantage?' she laughed. 'No one wants to be in a hospital on purpose.'

'Not even if it would bring me to you?' he asked.

'What kind of question is that?' she asked. 'I don't know who you are.'

'I don't want to play games, Emma.'

'*Games?*' she repeated.

'Yes. And this is not one you will win.'

'Everyone likes to win, don't they?'

'Some more than most,' he agreed. 'Some stack the deck in their favour. Hide an ace up their sleeve. They underestimate their opponent, and ultimately lose.'

'What are you talking about?' She blew out an exasperated breath and swept the hair out of her face.

He felt the pressure build in his chest until he was vibrating with it. Something feral. *Primal*.

She blinked up at him. 'Did you just growl at me?'

He moved closer to her, raised his fingers to her forehead.

'May I?'

'What are you doing?'

He stalled. 'I need to see.'

Eyes wide, she asked, 'See what?'

His fingers, feather-light, lifted her fringe.

'Emmy...' he exhaled and dropped his hands to his side.

'*Emmy?*' Her fringe fell, once again hiding the long graze on her left cheek and the ugly bruise on her forehead. 'Why would you call me that?'

'You *are* hurt.'

'I'm in a hospital—of course I am,' she snipped. 'But I'll heal. In time. Without medical intervention.'

'You said you fell?' He had to discern the lies from the truth.

'Yes. *I fell*. How many times do I need to repeat myself?'

'This will be the last time,' he promised. 'Tell me. What happened?' he asked, because he wanted to hear it. The detail. The rehearsed script written just for him.

Because there it was again, the doubt that coursed through his veins in sluggish waves.

Yes, she was hurt, he conceded. But she was using

it to get to him, taking advantage of the situation she had found herself in, he rationalised to soothe himself. But it did not soothe him. He was conflicted. And that was surely the point, exactly her intention: to confuse him enough that she could influence the outcome of their reunion.

'I've already explained what happened to the triage nurse, the doctor, the registrar...' She scowled. 'I suppose one more time can't hurt,' she said, and raised her knees.

His eyes followed the movement. And this time he really looked at the state his wife was in. Her tights were ripped, split like ladders on her knees. The rungs spread wider as her legs rose to her chest. And there was blood.

His heart thumped harder in his chest. He'd never seen her injured. Not even as much as a paper cut. And yet her knees were scraped raw. Her face... Her head...

'*I* was carrying too much.' She looked at the phone in her hand. 'I went to try and check the time on this.' She threw it on the bed. 'I lost my footing and went down with potatoes.'

'You went down *like* a sack of potatoes,' he corrected.

'No.' She shook her head. '*With* them. The taxi driver wouldn't help me carry the shopping up the stairs. I didn't want to leave the bags for an opportunist thief. I'm on the second floor of a maisonette so it takes time to get up the stairs. And now that's a week's worth of shopping ruined.' She grimaced.

'Such a waste. And it's horrible waking up to an empty fridge, which I shall be now.' She picked up the phone from her side and held it out to him. 'In fact, maybe you would be able to call my mum?'

'Your *mum*?' Shock pumped through him.

She looked at him quizzically. 'She doesn't work far from here. Just outside the city centre. She cleans for an agency.'

He hadn't known that. Emma had never told him anything about her life before they met. No details at least.

'She did?' he asked.

'Does.' Her frown deepened. 'Tonight's the library. After she's finished cleaning, she reads. Romance. She has the entire library to herself. She forgets herself. Loses herself in the stories, loses hours. But...'

Emma inhaled deeply, and he watched her chest rise in amazement. He'd truly believed that she'd planned this all out to convince him she was helpless, that she needed him because there was no one else.

But would she really use her mother's death?

What if she is helpless?

The doubts were more insistent now.

'But what?' he pushed.

'The nurse said she couldn't reach her...she'd call my next of kin on the list. But there is no one else. Just me and Mum.' She looked up at the ceiling. Squinting. She returned her gaze to his. 'If you could *try* to call her...' She swallowed, and he watched her throat tighten as if invisible fingers had applied pressure to the delicate tendons and were squeezing. *'Please.'*

And he felt it. The crack in his chest.

She really didn't remember her mum's death.

She was telling the truth.

He couldn't let himself consider exactly what that meant right now or why the pressure in his chest kept building.

And so he would tell the truth too.

'I can't call her.'

'Why not?'

'She's gone, Emma.'

'Gone where?'

'To…' Dante struggled for a word that was not too direct, but not too soft. 'Heaven,' he said, although he believed in no such thing. There was one life. One chance to live it. The end was the end.

Emma's mother was dead. Emma *was* all alone.

'What do you mean?' Her face contorted.

'She died over three months ago,' he told her, stating the facts as they were. 'A heart attack.'

'That is a cruel lie,' she choked out. 'I saw her this morning.' Her face twisted in confusion. 'Why would you say that? Lie like that?'

'It is the truth.'

'It is a lie,' she accused.

'It is not.'

'It has to be…' Her face blanched. 'Who the hell are you?'

'My name,' he announced, 'is Dante Cappetta.'

Frowning, she asked, 'Is that supposed to mean something?'

'It should,' he said, and watched.

'Why?' Confusion spread across her tightly drawn cheeks. 'Who are you to me?'

'I'm your next of kin.'

Her blue eyes narrowed. *'What?'*

'Your husband,' he clarified. And he loathed the raw edge to each word.

'My what?'

She stared at him open-mouthed, and he stared right back. Waited for the magic man behind the curtain to appear. But no one was there. She needed him, didn't she? No lies. No pretence…

'I'm your husband, Emma.'

'What kind of prank is this?' Anger churned in Emma's gut. 'You walk in here, tell me my mother is gone and proclaim yourself as—'

'Your husband,' he interjected smoothly.

'Is this how you get your kicks?' she spat. 'Do you roam around hospitals looking for vulnerable women? Do you convince them their only family is dead and prey on their tears?'

'You are not crying.'

Adrenaline burst inside her.

'And you're *not* my husband,' she continued, and choked on the absurdity of each syllable. 'You are nothing to me,' she finished, because it was the truth, the only truth she'd accept.

'I am your husband,' he said again.

She froze, not breathing, not moving. But her skin prickled. Her mind buzzed.

Her eyes travelled over the crisp, dark suit moulded to his body. A very *defined* body. The open-collared shirt beneath his jacket hugged his chest and revealed a thick, muscular throat.

She moved her gaze back to his face. Perfectly symmetrical, with high cheekbones, a powerful jaw and a noble nose. And his eyes were so dark, so deep, she could fall into them.

'It's impossible,' she breathed. Because it was. She didn't recognise a single inch of him. She didn't know this man. 'I don't have a husband,' she declared. 'I have never been, and never will be, married.'

'And yet you are married,' he contradicted smoothly. *Too smoothly.* 'To me.'

'Ridiculous!' she said, because it was.

Emma knew the truth.

She knew that love was not the fairy tale everyone said it was. She'd seen that first-hand, watched her mother wither under her father's supposed love.

Her mother and father had never married, but he'd used her like a wife when it suited him and mistress when he didn't.

She'd vowed long ago that she wouldn't give a man—*any man*—a legal right to any of her.

'Ridiculous?' he repeated. 'What is?'

'*You.*' She waved at…him. The entirety of him. And there was so much of him. He'd walked into her cubicle as if he had every right to be there. And when he'd demanded answers to questions she'd already answered, she'd thought nothing of it. He'd exuded the kind of confidence that you didn't think to question. She could see her mistake now.

Emma sucked in a fortifying breath.

'This very conversation,' she said. 'It has no basis in reality.'

'Why would *I* lie?'

'Are you insinuating *I'm* being dishonest?'

His eyes penetrated hers intensely. 'No,' he said roughly, and it crawled across her skin like a command for her body to react, to tighten. She dismissed it as an involuntary reaction because…he was consuming. His presence was stifling. And yet it soothed her too, in a way she couldn't understand.

'I'm not insinuating anything,' he said. 'Because you *have* forgotten who *you* are.'

'I know exactly who *I* am,' she snapped. 'My name is Emma Powell.'

His jaw hardened. 'No, you are Emma Cappetta.'

'Emma Cappetta?' she echoed, because she couldn't help it. And the name felt at home in her mouth. It shouldn't, she knew that. And yet, it did.

'Yes,' he confirmed. And she saw the flare to his nostrils, the swell of his chest. '*My* wife.'

Wife. He said it with such conviction. Such possession.

'I am nobody's wife.'

She would be no one's fool.

His fingers edged towards her, and she couldn't tell him to stop. Her vocal cords refused to cooperate because her body was so warm.

She found herself eager for his touch on her skin.

She must have bumped her head harder than she thought.

He claimed her left hand. 'Look,' he demanded, and dipped his head to where his thumb stroked her ring finger.

And she begged her body not to betray her, not to allow him the satisfaction of her obeying his whim.

'What am I meant to see?' she asked and met his gaze defiantly. 'Because all I see is a man touching a woman he doesn't know.' She snatched her hand away because it...*tingled*. 'Making absurd declarations!'

'You can feel it, can't you?'

'Feel what?'

She swallowed hard. A smile played on his lips, and there was an arrogance in his gaze. He knew that his ministrations had elicited a reaction quite unlike anything she'd ever felt before. And yet, it felt familiar too.

'The chemistry between us,' he answered, and the most frightening thing of all was the intensity of her body's response to the idea of him touching her again.

Maybe she'd knocked herself out completely and was still out cold. Maybe this was all a dream.

'The only fool in this room is you, thinking I'd believe we're *married.*'

His hand fell to his side. 'You may not be wearing your ring,' he said. 'But the evidence is there, if only you'd look.'

She closed her eyes. Counted to ten. *Slowly.* Surely she was going to wake up any minute now.

Any. Minute.

'What are you doing?' His question was spoken as softly as velvet brushed against her skin. His was a deep, sensual voice her ears liked, because they perked up, as did the speed of her heart, to a painful staccato rhythm.

And it was…*uncomfortable.*

Her mind didn't know him, but her body—

She opened her eyes. 'What am *I* doing?'

'Yes,' he replied.

'What are *you* doing?' she asked, hoping to challenge his deplorable confidence he belonged here, had the absolute right to touch her and call himself husband. When—

'Watching you.'

'Then stop it,' she spat, because his eyes on her felt…hot.

Her temples pounded. *Hard.* A bass drum between her ears.

She placed her fingertips to her temples and rubbed, but the pressure behind her eyes only increased. Her brain throbbed mercilessly, as if her mind was searching for something but an error code kept appearing.

'This isn't a movie,' she forced out. 'I didn't fall over and forget my life.'

'You have forgotten it,' he corrected. 'You have forgotten...*me*.'

'Who could forget *you*?'

'My wife, obviously.'

And she couldn't help herself any longer. She looked down at her ring finger. And that was when she saw it.

'Oh, my God.'

She brought her hand closer to her face. And sure enough, there on her finger was a tan line, a white circular band.

Just as he'd promised there would be.

Something had sat on her finger long enough for the sun to kiss the rest of her hand and leave this piece of her flesh untouched.

A ring.

'It can't be true,' she whispered.

'If you require it,' he said, 'I'll produce our marriage certificate.'

'Marriage certificate?' She flexed her fingers out in front of her again. 'Do you carry it around in your pocket for occasions such as this?'

Her laugh was a heavy cackle of self-mockery. Because what was a marriage certificate? Just a piece of paper. Her mother was, for all the intents and purposes, *married*. She'd had a child with a man she loved. She was devoted to him. Committed. But—

'I do not have the certificate here,' he said. 'But I do have this.'

His left hand appeared next to hers. On his ring finger was a plain, simple gold wedding band. And on the finger next to it, on his little finger, was another ring. It was an exact match to the first one, only smaller, more feminine.

He removed it and slipped the ring onto her finger.

She'd never thought of herself as a Cinderella wannabe. Never longed for that life. But this was her glass slipper, wasn't it? It was the perfect fit. A match. The white of her skin was hidden by the perfect circular thickness of gold on her finger.

It didn't feel...*wrong*. It felt as if it had always been there.

Her thoughts spiralled. Why would the doctor call for a psychiatrist when her wounds were physical? Why wouldn't they call her mum? Why did the nurse, the doctor, the registrar all look at her with pity when she'd explained she was twenty-two and living at home with her mum?

Because she didn't live with her mum anymore? Her mum was gone, and...she lived with him?

Who was the prime minister? What day was it? Was it Thursday as she thought it was? Was her mum reading in the library? Was she Emma Powell? Or was she someone else? Someone's wife? *His* wife?

Vulnerability threatened to close her windpipe.

But before it did, a warmth spread up her cheeks. This man, Dante Cappetta, was cradling her face. His hands were strong, and it made her feel...safe.

She couldn't explain it. The touch was so intimate. They were strangers in every sense in her mind. But her face felt *right* cradled in his palms, like it belonged there. And she didn't want him to let go, despite her logical mind knowing he shouldn't be touching her this way.

'You will come with me,' he said, his eyes shimmering with confidence that she'd go with him and let him take charge. 'You will see a doctor,' he continued, 'and be diagnosed with a plan of treatment within the next few hours.'

'I'm already in a hospital,' she reminded him.

His hands moved, releasing her face. His fingertips slid down her cheeks so softly, so *gently*.

Dante claimed her chin firmly between his thumb and forefinger. His eyes dark with determined decision, he proclaimed, 'We are leaving. Together. *Now*. This is the only choice. I will help you remember, Emma,' he promised.

'What if I don't *want* to remember you?' she asked, because someone—*something*—was lying to her, and if it wasn't him, if it wasn't her body, it was her mind, wasn't it? And the mind did things to protect the body. The soul. The…*heart*.

'What if my mind has blanked you out on purpose?' she asked. 'To protect me from *you*?'

'I am no threat to you, Emma,' he said roughly. 'We are married. I am your husband. Your protector. Trust me to protect you now.'

Marriage. Husband. Protector.

Those words did something inside her. Something she didn't want to recognise.

Physically, she was safe. He was no physical threat. She just knew.

He'd walked in here with no overt displays of emotion. He'd found out the facts and taken charge. Her mind didn't understand it. But her body…it *liked* it.

Everything felt uncertain. But his hands hadn't. They were steady. In control.

Realisation settled on her shoulders, in her chest. She would go with him.

'Okay,' she said, because right now he was her anchor to the truth.

In his world, she was his wife. And a part of her wanted to know what *that* life looked like.

'I'll come with you.'

CHAPTER THREE

IT WAS ALL TRUE.

Her mother was dead.

The grief was beginning to hit her.

She understood she'd lived through it already, even though she couldn't remember it, but it washed over her in waves.

It was a pain, an ache, an unfulfilled need all tied together in loops of barbed wire. And they sat in her ribcage now, all three side by side.

Her mother had been so young, with so much life left to live, and Emma didn't understand how a woman who had survived everything life could throw at her was gone.

Something tore inside her.

She looked down at the plain gold band on her finger. It was nothing ostentatious. It didn't scream wealth. Because it didn't need to scream anything, did it?

It was a symbol. The oxblood-red leather sofa seat groaned beside her as Dante sat. And the foot of distance between them evaporated in a millisecond when his hand reached for hers. His fingers slid between her own, entwining them together.

'Emma…' His thumb stroked the soft flesh between her thumb and forefinger. 'Are you okay?'

She pushed her bare toes into the thick carpet, halting the ridiculous urge to push her thighs together. He was touching her hand, for God's sake. Not anywhere intimate.

But it *was* intimate, wasn't it? His fingers entwined in hers meant she was allowing him to get close. *Too close.* And she wasn't sure she was ready for that.

She dragged her gaze up to his face and looked at him looking at her as if it were the most natural thing to do to comfort her. *Was* she comforted?

It didn't feel like reassurance. Her body was awake in parts she hadn't known were sleeping. Heavy and sluggish, but zinging as if she'd had too much coffee, as if she was overstimulated. Too sensitised. *Too awake.*

She tugged her bottom lip between her teeth. Comfort was something she provided for herself with extralong baths, or a trip to a shop to look at the pretty things that gave her pleasure she couldn't afford.

How had he convinced her to enter a relationship where holding hands was meant to provide comfort?

Emma did *not* hold hands.

'No.' Slowly, she withdrew her hand. 'I'm not okay.'

She eased her fingers out of his hold, resisted the pull to return it and stood.

She walked towards the back wall, which was covered from ceiling to floor with shelves of books.

This whole place was like a doll's house. It was the blueprint of every little girl's dream house.

'You *will* be okay, Emma,' he guaranteed too confidently.

She rounded on him. 'You can't know that.'

'But I can,' he contradicted her smoothly, 'because you are here.' He stood effortlessly. Moved towards her across some priceless rug. His every stride bringing him closer to her. 'With me.'

It took everything she had not to move backward. And what would be the point? There was a wall of books behind her. A dead end. She could move in another direction, but she didn't know this house. Didn't know the layout. All she knew was what was coming towards her.

She wasn't naive to the real reason heat pulsed in her abdomen.

It wasn't fear.

It was *want*.

She'd had encounters with men before. Fleeting and purely physical. She'd always found it easy to form a physical connection. To close her eyes and feel. Demand her body respond. Delight in momentary connections where she could take what she needed and walk away, emotionally untouched.

This time she hadn't demanded anything of this man.

And yet it was there. Stirring inside her. Making itself known. Something frantic. Something *consuming*.

'Do you always take charge so arrogantly?' she said, and she'd wanted it to come across as an insult dripping in sarcasm, but her words were breathless.

'Is it arrogance to give you what you need, Emma?' He looked so at home, he belonged against the backdrop of this house that most people would need to win the lottery to afford.

'Is it wrong to provide for you, my wife?' he continued silkily. 'To keep you safe? To make sure you never fall, that the load you carry is too heavy?'

Her heart snagged. Hadn't her load always been too heavy? She had been her mother's protector and her emotional support when she was far too young to be either.

That was why Emma had long ago made the safe choice never to become her mother. Never to be alone and waiting for a man, waiting for love. Never to get close enough to care, let alone *need* anyone. So, it was jarring to feel how soothing were his words that she didn't have to worry about those things. She felt a warmth spread through her.

'With me, they'll be no more empty fridges,' he declared, and his promise resonated with the little girl, the teenager, and the young woman who had *never* been promised an endless supply of food.

Her mum had worked endlessly to fill the fridge, but it had never been full for long enough. And when she'd got older, the cycle had repeated itself. Bigger bellies to fill, larger bills to pay, bills that were always overdue even when there were two pay cheques.

And here he was, promising these things as if they were nothing.

'Here, with me,' he said, 'you will have time, as the doctor recommended, to heal.' And his words were seductive. *Tempting.* 'Let me be clear—you are not a hostage. I'm not holding you against your will,' he said, his voice deep and warm. 'You can leave whenever you wish. But what better way to reclaim your memory than with me.'

The doctor had said her memory could return, or it might not. All she could do was wait and resume normal life.

Under the doctor's instruction, Dante had summarised her life for her. Five years delivered to her in a heartbeat. Impersonal and without detail. Only simple information. Milestones.

A move to London when she'd been twenty-two. They'd met when she was twenty-six, and their wedding had been the same year. The death of her mother was a little over three months ago, from a heart attack. And then she'd returned to Birmingham to pack up her mother's things, to attend her funeral, and then three months later, she'd fallen and hit her head.

And now she couldn't remember any of that.

She had the facts, sure. But what came between those facts? Why had she taken her wedding ring off when she'd gone back to Birmingham? Why had she stayed there? If her mother was dead, nothing was there for her.

She couldn't connect the dots. She and Dante

were married and yet, he was in Mayfair, and she'd been there.

Alone.

She twisted the ring that was back on her finger. 'Why did you have my ring?'

His face remained neutral. 'You left it behind when you returned to Birmingham.'

'Why?'

'Because you didn't want to wear it anymore.'

'What did I want?'

'To leave.'

'London?'

'No.' His jaw hardened. 'You wanted to leave me.'

'I wanted to leave you?' Her eyes grew wide. 'Why?' she asked again, because *why* was the word standing before every thought, and it flashed in neon green in her head.

'I don't know.'

'How can you *not* know?' she asked.

His lips thinned. 'You never told me.'

'I must have said something.'

'*"I want out."* That's all your note said.'

'I left a note?' she repeated.

Dante nodded.

'And you didn't ask for further clarification?'

'No.'

None of this made sense. *They* didn't make any sense. Not their marriage. Not their relationship. 'Your wife leaves her ring behind, tells you she wants out and you never thought to ask the reason *why*?'

'Why would I ask?' He shrugged. A nonchalant

dip of his broad shoulder. 'You left. The action required no further explanation.'

Tension threaded throughout her limbs.

Marriage was every commitment she'd never wanted, but she'd done it. For reasons unknown, she'd *married him.* And yet she'd walked away without a backward glance.

Her mother had never had the strength to leave her father. But Emma had left Dante.

Unbidden came the image of him with another woman. Her throat tightened against the wave of threatening nausea. Was that the reason?

Her chest seized.

Her lungs refused to function.

'Did you cheat?' she asked, because if he had cheated like her father had cheated on her mother countless times, she'd rather sleep on the streets than stay anywhere near him.

'Cheat?' he repeated, before closing the last few inches between them.

She prepared herself by pressing her heels firmly into the carpeted floor to steady herself for the impact of the vitriol that was surely headed her way.

But it didn't come.

'It has only been you,' he murmured as he tucked the loose hair in front of her left cheek behind her ear. His touch was delicate. Soft. And it took everything she had not to lean into it. Lean into *him.* 'Since the night we met, it has been only you.'

Blood flushed through her heart.

Air seeped into her lungs.

Only you.

The possessive sentiment scared her. Excited her.

Her mind wanted to reject his answer. Because how many times had she been told—*seen*—monogamy was a lie? Men always strayed. And yet here was Dante telling her that he hadn't.

'There *must* be a reason I left?'

'A reason you never shared with me.' He dropped his hand to his side. But he didn't remove the distance between them.

'If our marriage was over, why didn't we get divorced?' she asked, her mind still pulsing with the need to know, to understand… She'd dedicated a year of her life to their marriage and then walked away. Without saying goodbye. Without demanding a divorce.

'Does it matter?'

Her breath shuddered up her windpipe and out through her open mouth. 'Of course it does.'

'Why focus on the end of us when there was no end, no divorce?' he said. 'You left. We remained married. And now here we are. Together. *Again.*'

'Because of an accident,' she reminded him.

'Accident, fate, destiny,' he countered. 'Use whatever word you will, but you are here and so am I. So ask the right questions, Emma.'

'The right questions?'

'Questions I can answer without speculation.'

He was right, she realised. She could push and probe him for answers but only she knew, didn't she?

Why she'd married him. Why she'd left…they had both been her choices and hers alone, hadn't they?

'How did we meet?' she asked. He may not be able to answer the question of why she left, but there were other questions that he could answer.

'At a black-tie event. A charity auction, here in London. You were a waitress at the event and you collided with me,' he told her. 'Spilt your tray of wine. Wine that the hostess, the Princess of Vreotus, had donated from her very own vineyard.'

Emma expected self-consciousness to buckle her knees, because that meant the night they'd met she had been the help. But it wasn't self-consciousness making her knees wobble. It was desire, blooming inside her and swelling with every flick of his obscenely long eyelashes. Almost as if her body remembered what her mind could not.

'Place your hand on my chest.'

Frowning, she asked, 'Why?'

'I promised I'd help you remember,' he reminded her. 'So let me show you how it began between us,' he explained.

She lifted her hand. Touched him, tentatively.

'Can you feel it?' he asked.

Deep and steady, his heart thrummed beneath her fingers. 'All I can feel is you.'

He covered her hand with his and heat crept into her fingers. Up into her arms. Her chest. Until breathing became difficult. Too tight. Too shallow.

'And now?' he asked. 'What do you feel, Emma?'

Connection pulsed through her. A type of chaotic

harmony. An illogical knowing her hand belonged there. Beneath his.

'Heat,' she breathed.

'It is a flame,' he said, and his voice was rough. *Deep.* 'The night we met, when you raised your hand to my wine-drenched chest and touched me, right here, that flame ignited. Until it roared inside me. Unit it roared inside us *both*.'

Want pulsed inside her.

'Did we have a one-night stand?' she asked.

'We did. That night—' he leaned into her until their bodies stood millimetres apart '—and every night after,' he said.

It was difficult to focus her mind and listen to his story—their origin story—and reclaim it as her own lived experience. Especially when the compulsion to press herself against him, to touch him was clamouring for attention.

'Why did we get married?' she asked, her voice not her own. 'Why didn't we just have an affair?' she pushed, because she wanted to understand the choices she'd made. Because here she was, a girl from an industrial city who had moved from estate to estate when the rents were raised and they could no longer afford to stay. They'd had to relinquish their home so newer, younger, more prosperous families could move in with their two-point-four kids and domesticity.

A domesticity her mother had craved and Emma despised.

And yet here she was.

Domesticated.

'We did.' His breath feathered her lips. And she wanted to meet his breath with her own. Surrender her mouth up to his. *Kiss him.* 'Our affair lasted a month.'

Her fingers clenched at his shirt. 'What changed?'

'It wasn't enough.'

'What wasn't?' she husked. One night had always been enough. *For her.* An affair *should* have been enough. She still couldn't understand that.

'The stolen moments between us,' he said. 'I wanted no more borrowed beds,' he continued, 'however soft the sheets or exclusive the hotel. But a bed we could call ours.'

'And what did *I* want?' she asked, because she'd never shared anyone's bed for longer than was necessary. And no one had ever stopped her from leaving. They would feign sleep as she collected her things and disappeared without a backward glance.

But he'd wanted her to stay, to have a place they would meet and touch that was only theirs.

Had she wanted the same?

'You wanted me,' he said, and she heard it. Felt the unsaid part.

You want me.

'I asked you to marry me, and you said yes,' he finished. If she felt back then anything like she felt now, she could understand why she'd so readily agreed. Her body begged to be touched, to give in to the heat between them. To drown out the doubt, the questions.

A part of her still sensed there was more to the story of their marriage. But her mind was begging her in this moment to close the door on whatever that was. Because if everything he was saying was true, everything she believed about marriage—believed about herself—was a lie. It was simpler to believe that this really was about passion, desire and nothing more.

'There are so many unanswered questions,' she said, her fingers clinging to his shirt. 'And not knowing the answers to so many important questions... It feels like such a heavy thing,' she admitted, and her mind whirred with the heaviness. It pressed down on her sternum. On her lungs.

'It's okay to be scared, Emma.'

'I'm not afraid.'

'Liar,' he softly called her out, because he knew her, didn't he? And he was right; she was scared of the instinctive and knowing chemistry between them.

'But allow yourself to feel the anticipation of it,' he coaxed, and his words bloomed inside her ears. 'To be seduced by the unknown, to discover it piece by piece.'

The hand on top of hers moved to the base of her throat. His grip feather-light, his fingers skirted the flesh of her throat until the hilt of his hand met her chin, and lifted it.

'Allow yourself to feel the excitement of knowing the answers are coming.' Steady and intense, his gaze burrowed inside her. 'And embrace the journey of rediscovering yourself and our marriage.'

Dante was her only guide in these unfamiliar times. But his words, his advice, the connection crackling between their bodies, it was all too much. They made her tremble. They made her want all the things he'd told her she could have: financial security, protection, adventure. All in a home they shared, all because he'd put a ring on her finger and she'd let him do it. *Claim her.*

Emma's eyes travelled downward. Across the noble bridge of his nose to the dip above his top lip. It was the size of her fingertip and her hand itched to touch it. To smooth her finger across it to measure the indent.

Had she done that before? How many times had she tasted his mouth with her tongue, slipped her tongue between the slight opening between his thinner upper lip and fuller counterpart?

It was a mouth made for kissing.

Her insides tightened and squeezed on a breathless exhale.

With effort, she dragged her gaze away from his mouth to her hand which still sat against the hard muscle of his chest. It would be so easy to pull him closer, to surrender to instinct, use the fingertips clinging to his shirt to pull her closer and test how competent his mouth was.

She closed her eyes.

It felt reckless to put herself in his hands. To trust him to deliver his promises, when her logical mind told her his words were nothing but a seduction. *A lie.*

Her father had made countless promises to her

mother and delivered on none of them. But still her
mother had waited for the day he would keep his
promise to protect her. Emma. His family.

And now she was dead.

Emma understood she owed it to herself, and to
Dante, to rediscover their marriage. But marriage
felt so final. The end—*death*—to the woman she
thought she was.

Emma had had the courage to leave Dante once,
for whatever reason, but she hadn't been strong
enough to sever the tie between them completely.
That intrigued her the most. Had she been waiting
for Dante to return to her?

He'd said he wasn't holding her hostage, that she
could leave at any time, and that gave her a strange
sense of comfort. It softened the hard edges of her
fear.

And she felt the sudden need to confirm that his
intentions were true.

Emma opened her eyes. 'If I decide *this* isn't what
I want anymore…' Her fingers unfurled and splayed
on his chest, steadying herself.

But his hand stayed where it was beneath her chin,
keeping her head in position. Her eyes found his and
she held his gaze.

'At any time,' she continued, her chest tight, her
stomach in knots, 'you'll let me go, Dante,' she said.
Because she may not remember the version of the
Emma who'd married him, or why, and she wasn't
in a position to walk away right now, but she knew
twenty-two-year-old Emma would want this. How-

ever intensely she longed for his kiss, his body, *she* wanted an escape plan. In case she needed it.

'You'll give me a divorce?'

'Divorce?' Dante echoed, a slow, agonising breath flooding through his nostrils.

'Neither of us know the reason I left…*before*. But *I* did leave. And—' she swallowed, and he watched the delicate tendons in her throat constrict '—I want to give this life a chance,' she explained when he didn't speak. '*Us* a chance,' she corrected, 'to rediscover our marriage. I owe that to you, as much as I do to myself. But I need to know if I want to walk away, *again*, that it's really an option. That a divorce…'

'Will finalise the end between us?' he finished for her.

'Yes.'

Did she remember? Perhaps not all of it, but somewhere in that brain of hers she knew *that* was their way. The rules of their marriage, which was designed to have a 'get-out' clause. He could tell her about the rules of their marriage. *His rules.* The contract. But their contract had already expired. By every rule in the playbook, they should already be divorced. But they weren't. They were here. *Still married.*

And how did he explain that? Why he'd waited for the divorce papers to arrive. Why he hadn't initiated the proceedings himself.

He couldn't explain it. Not even to himself.

She was not his mother. She hadn't been looking

for a bigger payout. She hadn't been trying to gain the upper hand, wrestle back power.

Emma had left him by choice; he understood that now, but he also understood she'd come back to him because she had *no* choice. And she was right; not knowing the reason she'd left was a heavy thing. He ached with it too.

But did it matter? As he'd said to her, they could speculate, but it would amount to nothing but more speculation.

The truth of it was neither of them had demanded a divorce. They were still married.

But it was all she could see, wasn't it?

Marriage.

Everything she'd never wanted.

Until *him*.

He could tell her the truth of them, that they didn't do emotions, it was a marriage purely for passion, but why would he tell her? Ultimately those things hadn't made her stay before...

'If a divorce is what you require,' he conceded roughly, 'a divorce is what you shall have, Emma.'

'Thank you.'

'Of course.' He stroked the pad of his thumb along her jawline. 'Why would we remain married if we no longer wanted one another?'

'Exactly,' she husked, and he heard the unspoken realisation between them that divorce hadn't really been an option before because their marriage hadn't been over.

It still wasn't.

'I think I want to go to bed.' Her eyes glazed over, a mix of exhaustion and desire. His body reacted instinctively. His groin tightened. 'To sleep,' she clarified quickly. 'Alone.'

He didn't want to sleep.

He didn't want to spend a night in this house without her beside him. In his bed. In his arms. It was the reason he hadn't been back here since the day he'd found her gone.

His mind flashed with every moment he'd told her about. The beginning of them. The confident Emma who had touched him and met his mouth with the same ardent fever within moments of their first touch. The woman who'd embraced their physical connection as readily as he had. As if it gave them air. The woman who'd become his wife.

Every moment of their relationship had been borne from their physical connection. They never spoke about the past, what had made them the people who had met at that charity event. They'd only gone forwards, dived head-first into each other's body and stayed there.

Curiosity bloomed where it shouldn't. What made *this* Emma hesitate where she'd never hesitated before to welcome his kiss? His touch? Invite him into her bed? Any bed? What had happened to her between the ages of twenty-two to twenty-six to turn her into the woman he'd married?

He knew his wife. Every imperfection. Every sensitive spot. The spot behind her ear he let his breath heat and she would melt for him as he moved his breath, his lips, his mouth down and over her throat to her breasts.

But not…*her.*

In her mind they'd never kissed, never had sex.

It was all backwards. Upside down.

The urge to make her remember it all, to remember the feel of his mouth on hers, was overwhelming.

He knew she needed words. Needed reassurance before any of that. And he'd give it to her.

'Emma,' he breathed. 'Understand this. You're my wife. I'm your husband. This doesn't give me any rights to you. I won't take anything from you that you don't want to give. Everything I said stands whether you invite me into your bed tonight, tomorrow or never,' he said, because he knew that she needed to know in this upside-down world of theirs, she was safe. She had choices.

He dropped his hand and stepped away from her when his every muscle screamed for him to pull her to him, but he resisted.

Her head cocked to the side. She studied him silently.

'Do you understand?' he asked.

Jaw tight, she nodded.

'Use your words, Emma,' he said, because he needed confirmation that she understood she was safe with him. *Secure.*

'I understand,' she stated, but it wasn't enough.

'Tell me, what exactly it is you understand?' he pushed.

'That you'll look after me whether I return to

being your *actual* wife, or not.' She exhaled heavily, and he heard the tremble she was badly trying to conceal. 'I understand that whatever sexual relationship we had before it isn't expected from me now. That just because we're married, it doesn't affect anything. Because being married to you doesn't mean anything to me. *Yet.* It's nothing but a ring that fits. And if that never changes, you'll give me a divorce.'

He nodded, a tilt of his too-stiff neck. 'And for now, is that enough for you?' he asked, because he couldn't help it. He needed to know if the temptation of security would seduce her more than his lips.

'Yes.' She clasped her hands together at her midriff. 'It is.'

He stepped aside. 'Top door to the left,' he instructed. 'You will find our bedroom. *Yours,*' he corrected. 'Until you invite me to share it with you.'

And there it was. The dance between excitement and fear. The shimmer in her blue eyes. The pull tightening the skin on her cheeks. The tension in her shoulders threading into her muscles and lifting them.

'Good night,' she husked, and moved. She took a step forward, and another past him and ran.

He fisted his hands. The urge was so dominant to reach out to catch her.

He closed his eyes, denying the urge to follow his wife to bed.

He knew now what he hadn't allowed himself to acknowledge for the last three months.

He wanted her back. In his life.

He wanted Emma back, in his bed.

CHAPTER FOUR

ALL HER LIFE she'd refused to wait for anyone. But now she was waiting for him.

Emma's stomach whined. The pressure was too much. She felt too full, too empty at the same time. It was a void she knew no food could fill.

For two days, Dante had starved her of his presence.

He'd disappeared.

Gone.

Left her alone in their house.

Emma dragged her bottom lip between her teeth and bit down. Was this how her mother had felt like every time her father had promised her the world, every time he'd walked away and promised to return?

No, Dante was not her father. Dante hadn't promised her anything. He'd made everything a choice. It was her choice to stay or leave.

His words flooded through her now. The warmth of them seeped into her bones. The promise to take care of her. To wait until she was ready to explore *him*.

He had an effect on her without even touching her. Without being *here*.

She stared, unseeing, out of the port window onto the small airstrip below.

This was the reason she'd never wanted to be in a relationship. To be a woman who believed one day her prince would come.

Life wasn't one of her mother's romance books.

Emma could take care of herself.

Was she making the right choice to trust her gut? To stay? *To wait?* Was an escape plan enough to protect her? Because despite everything she knew, everything she'd seen her father do to her mother, the instinct was to wait for Dante. For her husband.

She'd run away from him the other night, up the spiralling staircase, through the door on the left, into the bedroom, because her body knew too much. *Wanted* too much. And that want was consuming her.

The private jet engines roared, a signal that the person everyone was waiting for was close.

The goldish-beige leather armrest surrendered to the pressure of Emma's fingertips, and it whimpered.

Dante stood at the end of the aisle aboard the private jet. He walked towards her, and he stole her breath. He wore a black shirt, open to his chest. Exposing his throat. His skin. He'd rolled up the cuffs, exposing his forearms too. Thick and strong, lightly spattered with dark hair. A black silver-buckled belt wrapped around his lean hips, accentuating the black fabric hugging his thick thighs.

She hadn't imagined it. She hadn't built up their

interaction in her head. He was everything her confused mind remembered.

He was the sun.

And despite everything, she wanted to run towards it, into its warmth.

The desire to do just that was primitive and loud. Her body screamed for her to stand, to meet him. And it felt so natural for her to want to surrender to the strength of her body's reaction to him, and forget the doubts, the questions, the *waiting*, and welcome him back with her lips on his.

He sat down beside her. Too close, and yet it wasn't close enough.

What was wrong with her?

He'd walked into the hospital and claimed her. Turned her world upside down. Turned *her* inside out and left her alone to sort out the chaos inside her.

'Emma,' Dante greeted, and her name was a caress. Pure silk. But it didn't soothe her. It chafed against her skin.

How dare he be so...*relaxed*? He'd kept her waiting. Hadn't told her where he'd gone or where he'd be. He'd just expected her to wait—*to be here*—and be happy when he came back.

And yet, wasn't that exactly what she'd asked of him—to allow her space.

A rage settled in her chest. 'Where have you been?'

He clipped himself in. 'In my hotel.'

She knew he was wealthy. But... 'Your hotel?'

'One of several hundred.' Dante signalled for the

plane to depart with a nod and a flick of his elegant wrist.

Emma's blood roared. 'Where are we going?' she demanded.

He didn't flinch. But he moved. His hands went to her waist and his knuckles brushed her hip bone, feathered across her stomach as he clipped her in. She swallowed down the rumble inside her, the gasp in her throat. She had been told this morning that they were going on a trip. But she had no more details than that. She'd been told nothing.

She hadn't even packed her own bags. Not that she would have even known what to pack. Nothing in the wardrobe felt like hers.

Dante sat back in his seat, observing her with quiet intensity. 'Japan.'

She arched a brow beneath her fringe. 'Japan?'

The jet taxied down the small airstrip.

'Tokyo.'

'And what's in Tokyo?'

'*We* will be—' his eyes flicked to the silver-faced watch on his wrist '—in twelve hours.'

His gaze moved over her face.

'Did you miss me, Emma?' he drawled.

Had she? Was that why she was so upset?

Her chest heaved. 'Is that what you wanted?' His hand fell to his lap, but his eyes never left hers. Brown probing blue. 'Was it a little revenge?' she husked. 'Is that why you disappeared without saying goodbye? Did you want me to feel what *you* felt when you found me gone three months ago?'

The tyres hummed along the tarmac. The speed, the adrenaline, fed her rage. And it felt good to be mad. Mad at life. Mad at *him*.

'Did you miss *me*, Dante?'

'In our old life, I would show just how much,' he said without missing a beat, and heat flooded through her. 'But why would I punish you for something *you* can't remember?'

Her chest was so tight she could barely breathe. 'Because *you* remember.'

The anger inside her was suddenly rising. So quick, so intense. Anger at herself. For wanting… for waiting.

'At least I left a note.'

As the jet ascended into the skies, his gaze moved over her face. 'Did you think I wasn't coming back?'

'I knew you would.' Her shoulders rose. 'Eventually,' she said, because that was what men did when you gave them the opportunity. Exactly what her dad did. Disappeared and returned when it suited him.

'And here I am.'

The arrogance.

'Is this what our life was like before?'

'Like what?'

'Do you leave me often?'

'I did not leave you. Besides, you are here,' he corrected, 'with me. Now.' He frowned.

'But did you keep me waiting for *you*?' she continued, because what was the alternative? To…accept that this was who she was now, a woman who waited around for a man? Her stomach curdled.

'I refuse to be a pawn in someone else's life, Dante.' She swallowed, but it didn't ease the tension in her throat.

Today, they'd packed her cases with clothes she had no recognition of. Escorted her into a waiting car. Organised her life for her. And she'd felt like a piece being moved on a board game where the winner was already known to all but her.

'Staff have moved me around today,' she continued, her voice heated. 'They packed my cases, delivered me to *you*—' Her chest burned and she breathed fire. 'I am not a parcel!'

'I'm sorry.'

She blinked. *'What?'*

He leaned in until their eyes were level. Until his breath fanned her lips. Until he was so close she could feel the heat radiating from his skin.

'I'm sorry,' he said again.

And her brain did not compute. She'd expected lies, expected him to try to absolve himself. She hadn't expected an apology.

'What are you sorry for?' she asked. She wanted an explanation. A *real* explanation. Because *sorry* was still an easy word to say.

'The Mayfair house has lots of bedrooms,' he said, his eyes never leaving hers. 'I could have stayed in any of those. But none of them are *our* room. I chose to stay in my hotel. I chose to leave and I chose to not wake you *or leave a note*—' his eyebrows rose '—to say goodbye. For *that* I am sorry. But I'd make the same choice again. Because staying in a room that is not ours, in the room next to you, as you sleep in our bed, in our house... It was too much. So I left. Because I understood—I *understand*,' he corrected. 'You needed time to find your footing in this life you don't remember, but I also needed time to find mine.'

She tilted her chin. 'Explain that to me.'

He shrugged, a nonchalant dip of his too-broad shoulder. 'My wife doesn't remember me. Our marriage. And when I brought you home from the hospital, being in the same house with you and not being able reach you...'

'Reach me?' she asked. 'I was right there.'

His lips flattened. 'I meant what I said, Emma,' he reiterated. '*All of it*. But it does not ease...'

'The reality of our situation,' she finished for him, and shame gripped her. She hadn't considered any of that. Only her own feelings. How *she* would navigate her way through this.

'Our relationship is starting...*backwards*,' he said. 'So we will start somewhere different. A different country. Different rooms. Different beds. In an environment where it will not be...'

'So hard?' she asked. 'Because in *that* house all you can see are memories of what we were before?'

'The house—' He grimaced. 'We don't need to be there to help you remember. Or find our...*feet*. We only need to be with each other. But away from the house...'

'It will be new for us both?'

He studied her face for a beat too long. 'Something like that.'

The jet levelled out.

'I'm sorry too,' she said, because she owed him an apology. She sighed. 'I was so wrapped up in navigating my amnesia for myself,' she explained, 'I hadn't contemplated how difficult this must be for you too. Because it's not just me starting again, it's both of us. I should have considered that. I should have considered *you*. And for that, *I* am sorry.'

'No apology required, Emma,' he dismissed with a raw edge to his voice. 'You were hurt—'

'I *was* hurt,' she interrupted. 'And you came for me. I appreciate you didn't have to. I left you without an explanation. You had every right to not come, but you did. And for that—' she swallowed tightly '—thank you.'

His eyes held hers and she couldn't catch her breath. Couldn't slow her pulse. He was right, wasn't he? There was something crackling between them. A heat drawing her in…

She dragged her gaze from his. 'You said you own hotels…' she said, forcing her attention to something real. Not the energy between them she couldn't see, couldn't understand. She peeked up at him from behind lowered lashes. 'Are you a hotelier?'

He shook his head. 'I'm the CEO and owner of a luxury travel company,' he replied.

'A travel company?'

'The Cappetta Travel Empire specialises in providing adrenaline-fuelled adventures catered specifically to each client. We provide the whole experience, transport, opulent accommodation and we plan their—' he shrugged '—their holiday for them.'

'You plan it for them?' she asked. 'Like tourist excursions?'

'The Cappetta experience is not an excursion, but an expedition into the unknown,' he corrected. 'It changes men, women, from the inside out.'

'Changes them?' She frowned. *'How?'*

'It depends on the client.' His eyes moved over her and her body tightened in all the places it shouldn't. His gaze moved back to her eyes. 'Expeditions vary from extreme sports, mountaineering, trekking through unmapped canyons to eat and sleep in places that shouldn't exist, and yet they do, Emma, because I've seen them.'

'And then they are changed?' she asked.

His eyes blazed. 'The Cappetta experience gives the mind the right tools to jump out of an aeroplane when the ultimate fear is heights,' he explained. 'It teaches the mind to allow the body to be free. To reach a higher plane of existence. To...*transcend*.' His lips lifted.

Her stomach somersaulted. Is that what he'd done to her—given her the tools to take what she needed from what she feared most? *Marriage?*

'And who gave you the tools to teach others to live this way?' she asked.

'My grandfather. He was a pilot. He built a domestic airline to respectability. My...father.' He swallowed and she watched the heavy drag of his Adam's apple. And she recognised it. Heard the tension around the word *father*. The difficulty in saying the word.

'Your father?' she said, curiosity taking hold.

'He was many things. Pilot. Captain. Adventurer. He travelled the world on any mode of transport that brought him to his destination. To a place that fulfilled whatever particular need he had at the time,' he replied, and the shadows were gone from his eyes. His face a mask of unreadability. 'He revolutionised his father's small domestic airline into a travel empire with a backpack and a blog when the Internet was in its infancy. Others wanted to experience his way of life. His ceaseless desire to...'

'Transcend?' she offered.

'Indeed,' he said. 'So my father adapted his methodology for travel, for individual needs, and at maximum profit.'

'And your dad taught you?' And she watched for the shadows. But nothing came.

He shrugged. 'It is in my blood.'

She wanted to understand this nature of his, how it had tempted her into becoming someone unrecognisable.

'But I'm no longer on the ground arranging expeditions,' he continued, and she saw the pulse spike in his cheek. 'Unless *I* want to.'

'Unless you need the...*rush*?' she asked, because she couldn't imagine this choice of his, to live life how he wanted to. *Dangerously.* A life where the aim was nothing but to feel good. Not just good but...*alive.*

'I need it,' he confessed. 'The adrenaline. The rush of excitement. It's my job. A way of life. But I don't need to be on top of a mountain to feel it.' Her eyes flicked to his. 'It's possible to find it in…other areas.'

Her pulse surged. *Painfully.* She pictured the bed she'd spent two days in alone. But what of the other times she'd slept in it? With him?

'Is that what our marriage was like? Adrenaline fuelled? Thrilling? *A rush?*'

'It was,' he said, his gaze obsidian. 'And we needed more. *Always.* We were both powerless in the face of its ferocity.'

She didn't drink alcohol. Hadn't for a long time. But she remembered the effect it had on her body. The haze—*the fog.* And she was swimming in it now.

'Sex,' he said, and her heart stopped. The word *sex* slipped from his tongue as if it were the most natural word to use to define them. 'It was wonderful between us. It was the rush we both craved and the high we found in each other.'

'You make us sound like adrenaline junkies,' she said. 'Or sex addicts!'

'We were both,' he confirmed. 'And all it took was one passionate kiss and we were lost to each other.' His brown eyes burned black. 'Addicted.'

She'd never been addicted to anything. Never wanted anything more than once…

She'd had sex before. But *passion*?
Never.

Sex was sex. She enjoyed it. *Sometimes.* But all in all, it was a perfunctory physical release.

Her eyes dropped to his lips. And the urge was stronger than it had been two days ago. It was all she could think about—how his mouth would feel on hers.

She wanted to taste it. *Test it.* This rush he spoke of. This high.

Just once…

Months of self-denial heightened Dante's senses. They blazed when they saw the pure intensity with which Emma was staring at his mouth. And she was moving. *Slowly.* A millimetre for every heartbeat. Every breath.

His every primal instinct demanded he draw her in to his chest. Crush those lips of hers to his.

He'd spent the last two nights thinking of those lips. Their softness. How he'd stood before her wondering if she would act on the impulse that they'd both shared. But she'd resisted then. She'd walked away. Gone to bed. *Alone.* He'd wanted to stalk her. Up the stairs. Into bed. *Their* bed.

He knew he'd promised her that he would let her take the lead. But it didn't ease the ache, didn't ease the ferocity with which he wanted her.

Selfishly, he'd known if he stayed in *that* house with her, he would have waited for an opportunity to strike. To graze his mouth along the sensitive skin of her throat.

He wouldn't have been able to stop himself touching her when he'd promised he wouldn't. And Dante kept his promises. He'd promised he'd wait.

But the waiting had already been too long. He ached with waiting.

But this wasn't the Emma who tore the buttons off his shirt to feast her lips—her tongue—on his bruised nipple. This wasn't the Emma who had needed nothing but his lips on hers. His body on her. *Inside her*. This was not the Emma who understood the unrestrained physical desire which had led them to the altar.

She was a different Emma. A woman who demanded to know his whereabouts. *Their* destination. When the only thing *his* Emma had cared for was how long it would take them to get to bed. *Any* bed. The wall. The floor...

This Emma and her questions, she made him question everything, including the way they had existed before.

Did he treat her like a pawn? Did he move her into position to welcome him back? Did he leave her behind?

Yes. But he *always* came back. Such were the rules. Such was their marriage.

These questions made his skin itch.

The plan he'd made had been simple. And it remained unchanged. There was no need to change it. Even with all the questions.

He'd seduce her with all the things he hadn't needed the first time. He'd treat her like a client. Cater this work trip around her. Show her a side she'd never seen of him. A side she'd never needed to see before because they'd been playing by a different set of rules.

But now, the rules had changed. And he'd use all the tools in his arsenal to bring back the status quo. He'd dazzle her with his lifestyle. With this jet. With Japan. The opulent life only he could give her. A life where the thrill came first. A life she could only live with him.

Emma might not remember, but he knew what she wanted. *Him.*

And he could see his plan was beginning to work already. She was returning to him, remembering their connection… She'd be in his bed by nightfall.

Triumph roared through him.

He sat very still.

He wouldn't coax.

He wouldn't push.

He didn't need to.

She was in charge.

And he knew that when once she felt his mouth on her there would be no going back for her. No escape. Because there hadn't been for him.

He waited, holding his breath, waited for Emma to deliver herself to him.

Her blond hair sat on her shoulder in a low-slung ponytail. Her burned orange shirt and ankle-length olive-green skirt sat against her pale skin with the vibrancy of autumn.

Her mouth was a hair's breadth away from his now. And Dante couldn't help it. He leaned in. Not all the way. But enough to push past any defence she had left against the current coursing between them.

Her lashes fell over her eyes. And then there was no space. No distance between them.

It was only the lightest touch of her lips against his, but need ripped through him. Dominating him.

Dante thrust his tongue in her mouth, meeting her need with his own.

All the blood in his body flowed to his groin in a tidal wave of heat.

It overwhelmed him now. Not only the need to taste her, but the warmth spreading over him as her hands held his face, pulled him closer. Invited his tongue to thrust deeper.

The feeling was familiar.

He'd felt it when the snow and the winds had pummelled his body as he climbed the highest peak in the Himalayas. When he'd been stuck between the summit of Everest and the base below.

Exhausted, but exhilarated.

Nature had tested his limits. His resolve.

The freak storm had hit, and no one had seen it coming. Without visibility, there had been no way of following the rope back to camp. His oxygen tank depleting, he'd sheltered as best he could. He'd found a ledge and stayed there. Waited it out.

It was the closest he'd come to death. And afterwards, after the storm had passed and the adrenaline had subsided, he'd craved warmth. Human connection, the need to know he wasn't alone. It was a feeling that he'd found unwelcome. He didn't need anyone.

And he felt it now.

That need for *warmth*.

Emma's warmth.

Shock hardened him. His every muscle. His forearms strained not to hold her too tightly. The muscles in his chest held him back, restraining his every urge to push against her.

He'd needed no one. Never risked being emotionally involved to the point when someone could leave him. Abandon him. Emma had done all of those things. And yet, kissing Emma after so long…

Had he become emotionally attached to his wife? So attached that she was part of his survival?

The realisation was too much.

He did not want her warmth.

He wanted her heat.

Her sex.

He kissed her harder. *Deeper.* He thrust his fingers into her hair, tilted her neck to gain deeper access and he punished her mouth with his own. With his tongue. His teeth.

'Dante…' she panted, and he drank from her mouth. He kissed her with everything pulsing inside him. His wants. His needs.

But there was something else inside him. Something he didn't want.

Regret.

Regret his lips hadn't kissed hers for too long. That he'd abandoned his duty to maintain this fire.

Worked, *maybe* too much, when he should have been kissing her. Keeping her hot, ready and wanting.

Was that why she'd left?

It didn't matter.

She was here.

In his arms.

His thumbs found her pebbled nipples beneath her blouse and stroked. Brushed them with the pads of his thumbs. But it wasn't enough. He wanted them in his mouth. He wanted to suck. Tease. Until the hardened peaks pulsed between his lips.

He moved his fingers to the pearl buttons of her shirt and began to undo them. He did not release her mouth. He suckled her tongue. And she mewed for him.

He needed to know her again. Feel the suppleness of small breasts in his palms. He needed to taste her. Her skin.

His hands moved, unclipped their belts and then went to her hips, pulling her closer. Into his embrace.

Her breasts pushed against the white lace that held them in place, pushed into his palms. And he needed to be naked. He needed Emma naked. Skin on skin. He needed to be inside her.

He wrenched fabric between his fingers until he was scrunching it, pulling up her skirt—

'Stop!' She pushed at his chest. Tore her mouth from his. Firm fingers on his chest held him at bay. But her pupils flared into black disks. They told him the truth. She didn't want to stop.

She wanted him. So why?

Panting, they stared at each other.

Something unfamiliar wound itself around his shoulders and pushed down. Why was she not smiling? Sliding over to him with open arms so he could pull her onto his lap? Undo his zip and release himself for her pleasure? For his? One kiss was all it had taken before…

'I want to…' She looked at her hands on his chest, and her mouth twisted. She pulled her hands away. 'Talk,' she announced, her breath coming in short, sharp rasps.

'Talk?' His mind raced. They did not *talk*. They did not stop their love making for a chit-chat break. 'About what?' he asked raggedly.

'Us,' she breathed. 'You. *Me*… I don't remember the marriage we had, but I want to know. I want to learn. I want to know my husband better.'

'Are you not learning, Emma?' he asked. 'What I taste like? How it feels to have my tongue in your mouth and my hands on your body?'

A blush bloomed up her throat to kiss her cheeks. She shifted on a heavy exhale and stared fixedly ahead. Spine straight. 'I want to learn who I was, who I am, who you are, without—' she swallowed '—*this*. Without this complicating things.'

'"*This*"?'

Her gaze met his. 'This urgency between us. It's too frantic. It's too—' She looked down at her shirt and began to do the buttons back up. 'It's too…*indecent*.'

'Indecent?' he growled, because *his* Emmy would be between his thighs taking him into her mouth.

And he ached for his wife's lips.

'It is not indecent to want my wife. To want you naked. To feel your thighs squeeze against mine as you take me inside you.'

He saw her blush.

'Enough.' She shook her head. *'Please.'*

And he was on that ledge again. Alone and waiting.

They both remained silent but for the heaviness of their breathing.

'Is there somewhere to sleep?' she asked.

He nodded. He knew she was running again.

But he also needed her to leave, didn't he? So he could lick his wounds. Replan his attack. His seduction. Because somehow his reaction to her kiss—her rejection—was affecting him in ways he didn't like.

He buzzed for an attendant and requested she take Emma to the plane's master suite. Emma stood to follow the smiling attendant.

'Dante?'

He looked up into her face. His eyes lingering on the swollenness of her lips after his kiss. And he wanted to reach out and touch her mouth.

He fisted his hands on his thighs.

'I look forward to getting to know you in Japan,' she announced, and turned on her heel.

Never had Emma walked away from him. Shut him out. Physically not wanted him close. And now she'd done it twice.

He couldn't fathom it. They'd never talked before. He'd learned more in the hospital room a few days ago than he had in a year married to his wife. Her mother, her job, the empty fridge. And he had more questions than he'd ever imagined.

How often had the fridge been empty? How many jobs had her mother worked? How many had Emma worked over the last three months? Had the fridge been empty again?

He scowled. Because these things…what did they matter? He wanted his wife back. What was there to know that he didn't already?

But it weighed on his conscience.

Had Emma wanted more? More of his time? More conversation? Would he have been open to talking if she'd asked him? Was he open to it now?

It was captivating, wasn't it? This change in his wife. The idea of seducing her without sex was…

A novelty.

An intriguing one.

He rolled his shoulders.

It was a challenge he'd welcome.

And win.

CHAPTER FIVE

EMMA STEPPED ON to the terrace of their hotel suite and embraced the light breeze on her skin.

It had been two days and she could still feel heat clawing at her. It was the only thing she understood about her relationship with Dante. She couldn't make sense of anything else but that, which was why she'd asked him to stop. Before they'd headed to bed, any bed.

Shinjuku City was spread out before her. She'd seen the lights from the highest floors of every skyscraper that required a cleaner, or a silver service waitress, but she'd never seen…*this*. She'd been raised in a city, but this was unlike anything she'd ever seen.

This was a city made up of buildings piercing the clouds, a city that kissed a mountain. Any minute now, the sun would move again and settle behind Mount Fuji.

She pressed her open palms to the balcony balustrade.

They hadn't talked. They'd moved into the penthouse mansion two days ago and she hadn't set eyes on him since.

She'd drawn the battle lines, and he'd retreated with the excuse of touching base with the board of his company. She understood what he was doing.

His vulnerability on the plane had been raw. As open and present as her own. He missed his wife. But she wasn't his wife. At least not the one he remembered. *Not yet.*

And he remembered everything. Their first kiss. Their every touch. Every night spent in their bed together.

But she still had the same questions. Why had she married him in the first place? Why had she left? And her only goal was to figure it out. To figure *him* out. To learn, to understand, who she was with him. The only way to do that was to talk without the urgent pressure of his lips. Because, on the plane, she'd felt the adrenaline, and the need to chase it.

It would have been so easy to fall beneath him, and stay there, under the weight of him. Far too easy. But sex didn't feel like a big enough reason for her to marry him. To tie herself to a man legally. No matter how intoxicating his kisses, or how good he made her feel.

He hadn't spoken of love. And for that, she was grateful. She didn't want it. She didn't want him to love her, and she did not want to love him, did she? But then what did *that* mean? What kind of marriage did they have if it wasn't based on love?

Was their marriage really just based on sex? And

if that were true, if that was what twenty-six-year-old Emma had wanted and agreed to, why had she left him when the chemistry between them was so potent?

Had Dante wanted more? Had she walked away from her marriage because she couldn't give to him the kind of marriage her mother had craved? Did he want a family? Children? Did he still want those things? Was that why he'd come for her? Was that why he hadn't divorced her? Because he still hoped he could persuade her?

She swallowed. Had she not divorced him because she too hoped that he would change his mind? Or perhaps because she had fallen for him...

She felt his presence before she heard it. A shift in the air, in her.

'Have you been bored without me, Emma?'

She didn't turn. Didn't visibly let her body react, but the deep husk of his voice reached inside her.

The instinct to turn and move towards him was overwhelming. All she wanted was to meet him. To raise her mouth to his in invitation and demand he kiss her again. Kiss her until all she could feel, all she could question, was how to angle her mouth. Until she was breathless with his kisses.

She closed her eyes to steady herself. She couldn't do any of that, not until she understood why she'd married this man who made her blood run hot, whose kisses left her frantic, who made her feel unaligned with her natural self.

'How could I be bored with this view?' She

opened her eyes and commanded her gaze to stay forward, on the glints of orange disappearing into the shadow of the night.

'It's beautiful,' he agreed, and in her peripheral vision, she saw his hands slide onto the balustrade next to hers.

'If you listen carefully,' he said, 'you will hear the ring.'

'The ring?'

'The bell of a setting sun.'

She listened. Watched as day turned to night. Heard the bell as the sun disappeared into darkness behind the mountain.

Slowly, the lights flickered on in every window, on every street, and the city was ablaze with artificial rainbow light, the mountain hidden until tomorrow. But she knew it was there. Even in the shadows. An impenetrable force of nature. Just like Dante. There even when he wasn't. In her mind. Intruding on her every thought…

She forced herself to relax.

'Was it always this way for you?'

'What do you mean?' he asked as she fought the urge to move close, to allow their elbows to meet, to allow the electric current to flow from her body into his.

No. Desire and discussion were to be separated.

'I mean with your dad. His job. Your grand-father's. Was life—' she waved at the cityscape '—always so spectacular?'

'It was,' he answered. 'It is.'

'Did you ever crave something simple?' She swallowed. 'Something less… Something more normal?'

'I have never known…*normal*.' He spoke softly, but his voice was laced with something heavy.

'I'm normal,' she countered, because she was. And she wanted to know why this extraordinary billionaire had married her.

What did they have in common?

She didn't know what she'd told him about her past or what he'd told her. But she'd start at the beginning, as he had when he'd told of their first meeting. She'd tell him the beginning of *her*.

'My life isn't unsimilar to many others,' she started. She didn't look at him, because it was easier to have this conversation without the intensity of his gaze boring into hers.

'I grew up hating my father and making sure I was always there for my mother, because he never was. I didn't grow up watching sunsets in penthouses made for the ultrarich and royalty. I grew up taking care of my mother. Supporting her so she could look after me. I helped her clean for her agency work before school. I'm the definition of normal. A city girl from a council estate, yet now—'

'You are here,' he interjected softly.

The rational part of her mind told her to tread carefully, not push too hard too soon, but she needed to know more.

'Did you hate your dad too?'

'What gives you the impression I hate my father?' he asked, and still, she didn't look at him. Didn't acknowledge the closeness of him, or the pull inside her to be closer.

'On the plane,' she confessed, 'there was a hesitancy when you spoke about him. A hesitancy I recognised because I feel it too. This conflict inside me when I think of him. That I owe him something because of his biological contribution to my life, all while hating him,' she hissed. And she waited, for the gasp. For his shock at how she felt about the man who gave her life.

Emma and her mum had had so many arguments about it. His behaviour. His treatment of her. And her mother had told her to accept that he still loved them.

But nothing came from Dante. Only silence and an invitation for her to continue. So she did.

'I know it sounds violent,' she confessed, 'but he makes me feel violent. Because I hate how she accepted his lies as truth. I hate what he did to her. What he turned her into. My mum—'

His hand moved then, atop hers, and she couldn't continue. Couldn't concentrate on anything other than the feel of his palm on her skin. His offer of comfort was given without her having to ask for it.

'What did he turn her into?' he asked, and this time she didn't look, because she didn't want to see pity in his eyes.

Had she ever told him what her dad had done? Why *he* was the reason she never wanted to marry? Why she found it hard to accept that someone would want to make her life easier?

'A doormat,' she rasped the truth of it. 'And however, many times I wanted to tell him to be gentle, to at least wipe his boots before he stomped on her again, she hushed me. Told me to be quiet. To accept that my...*father*,' she said, even though he was no such thing to her, 'would never be the man either she or I wanted him to be. That he would continue to break every promise he should have held dear.'

Emma tried and failed to keep the venom out of her voice. 'He seduced my mother when she was sixteen, promised he'd marry her but never did. He lied. And still, for all the years afterwards, she believed one day he would.'

Her heart ached for her mother. For that teenage girl who believed in the fairy tale, believed love would conquer all. Regardless of how much time passed, how many lies he told her, she believed in their love, in him.

'He abandoned her when she fell pregnant with me. He didn't come back even when she begged him to, even when she was kicked out by my grandparents. Even when I was born...' It was Emma who was hurting now, remembering that little girl who couldn't understand why her father didn't want her. 'He didn't come for a year. And then he only stayed for two days before leaving us. I have seen the pictures of him holding a one-year-old, his daughter, a daughter he'd only just met.'

She was breathing so hard, so fast, her words tumbled out of her. Out of a place she'd hidden them for so long it hurt to speak them. But she needed him to understand her hesitancy to accept their marriage at face value.

'And then there was another picture when I was five. Another when I was thirteen where I'm looking at him with disgust. And he disgusts me still. Not because he wasn't there for me. He wasn't there for *her*. Because every time he left, he promised he'd be back for good next time. But he couldn't be the man my mother deserved.'

Tears of rage clouded her vision but she wiped them away.

'He didn't deserve her. Her kindness. Her patience. Her devotion. He broke her heart and killed her with his lies.'

She turned and finally met the gaze she'd been avoiding. But there was no trace in his eyes of the pity she feared. But not empathy either. Just his steady gaze on hers. And his hand remained where it had the entirety of her story. On hers. Unmoving. Just *there*.

'That's why, on the plane, I was so angry. Angry that you'd left what was meant to be our house. In that moment, I was her—I was my mother.'

Her heart was beating so fast. So hard. And she felt vulnerable. *Exposed.*

'I swore I'd never be her. Never devote myself to any man. But I married you. And I... I need to understand it. I need to know who you are and that you're not him. Not like my father. That I have not betrayed myself and everything I stand for. That's why I stopped you,' she admitted rawly. 'Because it was too intense. Too blinding. Too frantic. Our marriage, it seems the antithesis to all that I am.'

She pulled her hand from beneath his and turned her body to face him. She'd never told anyone about her parents, and how their relationship had changed her forever.

She'd thought it would feel weak to have told him everything, but it didn't. It felt like she'd taken her power back, after amnesia had taken everything from her. She was choosing to share these memories with him.

'So help me to make sense of our marriage, Dante,' she said. Shoulders back, head raised, she continued, 'Talk to me. Tell me who you are,' she breathed heavily. 'Tell me why you hate your dad too.'

Dante gave a slight shake of his head.

For two days, he'd stayed in his company's Tokyo headquarters, avoiding this conversation. Talking wasn't how he had imagined he was going to persuade Emma back into his bed. And so he'd plotted how he'd exploit this talking she wanted to his advantage. And he'd planned to exhilarate her senses and distract her with worldly things. Sights and sounds that would make her dizzy.

He saw no advantage here. Only emotion and feelings. Feelings that he didn't want to examine, either hers or his own. He did not want to examine the faults of their fathers and find common ground.

They didn't need any here.

Only in bed.

And yet, it was clear that Emma would not be appeased by what he had been willing to offer. So he must adapt, change tack, offer…something.

'My life was not hard, Emma,' he said dismissively. 'I never worried about my parents' relationship. They didn't have one. I didn't worry about the bills or the fridge. I did not work before my tutelage. I never worried who would take care of who. My father employed a triage of nannies to care for me while he conquered the world.'

And women, he added silently.

'Your dad left you alone too?' she summarised without his permission. 'Left others to care for you while he cared only for himself?'

'It was not like that,' he said, but even as he did, he knew it was a lie. 'When I was of age, I conquered the world myself, and with him, guided by his ethos for life.'

'Isn't that what I'm doing—what I *did* before you?' She screwed up her nose. 'I let my father's *ethos* for life determine my every relationship. I didn't have relationships because I didn't want to be…'

'Abandoned?'

And it hit him now; the very thing she didn't want to happen to herself, she had done to him. Done to him what his mother had too. His father was different; he had never abandoned Dante, never made any promises.

He was your father; he shouldn't have had to. He should have just been there.

'Yes,' she admitted, jolting him back to the present. The spaghetti strap of her dress fell over her bare shoulder. He swallowed as her fingers grazed along her skin to pull it back into place.

'He never considered how him coming in and out of our lives affected us. It sounds as if your dad did the same,' she concluded, and his lips thinned into a firm line when she didn't stop. 'He gave you up to nannies until he could benefit from your company. He only showed up when it was of some benefit to *him*.'

She didn't understand his life.

She didn't understand him.

'It is not the same,' he rejected.

'Isn't it?' she asked, her blue eyes seeking and finding his. Something heavy shifted inside him.

'Why would I hate him, Emma?' He stepped closer to her, because how could he not? 'Everything I have. Everything I am, is because of him.'

And she looked at him now as if he was the source of her pain. And his feet halted. And he didn't like it. Didn't want it.

The story she'd shared with him, the relationship between her parents, it was everything they weren't.

In the past, he would have reached for her. Placed his hands to her waist, allowed them to slide down the cotton of her blue polka dot dress. Over her hips. Down her thighs. Seeking the hem at her knees. And he'd have taken her with her back pressed into him as she looked out at the view. Thrust inside her again and again, until all she could think, all she could say, was his name as she screamed it into the night. He would have turned pain into passion.

He fisted his hands.

He couldn't do that. Not yet, not with this Emma.

'Is that why you resent him?' she asked quietly.

'Why would I resent him?' he asked. Because it wasn't true, was it? 'You are looking for a common ground between us where there is none,' he growled. 'I am very much who I am because of my father. Because of the way he lived.'

'I loved my mother. She was there for me unconditionally, but I resented her too, for the way she lived,' she confessed, and he heard the crack in her voice. Heard how hard it was for her to admit. 'Her inability to let my dad go. It wasn't just my dad who changed my relationships with people, it was *her*. She made me so afraid, I'd...' She looked away from him and into the night. 'I'd let someone I—' she turned to him and her gaze was shuttered '—loved, take and take, until I was nothing more than a shell.'

Love? Did she think she'd loved him? That he'd loved her? That their marriage was based on all those emotions he didn't want and didn't know how to feel? She was no different; that was one thing he did know. That was why they were perfect for one another. No emotional attachments. Only physical desire. *Only want.*

Was that what she was afraid of? Was that why she had needed him to tell her that divorce was an option? That if she wanted to leave, she could? She needed an out in case the reason she had left before was because she had become emotionally invested in their relationship.

She wrapped her arms around her waist. 'Do you think all children grow up to be replicas of their parents?'

'Maybe,' he said. 'Why?'

'After all those vows and promises I made to myself, I wonder if I was always destined to…'

'Continue her legacy?'

'Yes.' Her eyes narrowed. 'Was it something in my DNA that I couldn't run from? Hide from…? The same way you couldn't hide from your destiny to continue your father's legacy.'

He didn't contradict her. DNA was undeniable. He was his father's son, after all. He knew the pressure of living up to a legend. He knew the worry of not being good enough.

For Emma, he supposed, it was the opposite. She didn't want to live up to the legacy.

'My father's dead, Emma,' he said, wanting this to end. 'I think of him little.' He shrugged off his suit jacket and took another step towards her. 'He was an uncomplicated man. He lived to live, took what he wanted from life, until he died.'

'He died?' she whispered.

He moved closer. 'He did.'

'How did he die?'

'A solo adventure on the high seas,' he told her. 'His boat returned—' he splayed his empty hand, palm side up '—empty.'

'I'm sorry.'

He moved closer still. 'Don't be. It was a death my father would have applauded.'

She gasped. 'Applauded?'

'An adventurer dies adventurously.' He shrugged. 'It would have been the way he'd have wanted to go.'

'On his terms?' she grated.

'Is that not the best way to live?' he countered. 'And to die?' And he watched the flare of her nostrils. The tightening of her bare shoulders. In her mind all men were the same, weren't they? Selfish even in death.

Was Dante selfish? Was she right to think so? Had he only kept her, kept coming back to her, for his own needs?

Of course he had, but he'd met her every need as well as his own.

'And your mother?' she asked, her eyes fixed on his. Watching. *Waiting* for whatever it was she was seeking in his answer.

'My mother,' he said, unsure how to take this conversation forward. How to expose bits of himself he never had before. To find this common ground he knew they didn't have. 'My mother has no influence in my life.

'Why not?'

'She gave birth to me and left to start a new life.' Something hot and unknown bubbled in his chest. 'She was out the door as soon as they cut the umbilical cord.'

She shivered again. 'Without you?'

'I had my father.'

'Sounds to me like you had no one,' she said. He could see the goosebumps covered her flesh now, highlighted by the soft amber lights flooding the terrace. She was cold. And he knew several ways to warm her. None that she wanted.

She was right, wasn't she?

He'd always been alone.

Until *her*.

He dropped his jacket over her shoulders and held on to the lapels.

'And now we have each other,' he said, and he knew it was a lie. They'd had each other for a time. A time until he didn't want her. Or she didn't want him.

The silence was palpable.

He felt it. The shift. The rise in her shoulders. The absence of breath leaving her lips.

He resisted the urge to thrust his nose into her hair. Grip the hair caressing the flesh between her shoulder blades and draw her to him. Kiss the exposed flesh beneath her ear and taste her. Move his mouth down her neck and bite the delicate flesh of her shoulder. And step back into familiar ground. To take them both back. Back to the beginning.

But there was no *back*, was there? Only this. Only now. Only *her*.

And he'd agreed to her demand of no more kisses, even when that was all he desperately wanted to do. To close the distance between them.

To sink into their connection. A deep connection that was always there beneath the surface.

A connection to something he couldn't see. Nature. *God*, maybe.

It was just there.

Humming.

And it was too loud. Too much.

But he wouldn't allow it to happen. Couldn't.

A kiss without heat.

He did not want her softness.

He didn't need it if it was not given freely.

He pulled away from her.

'Go to bed, Emma,' he commanded roughly.

'To bed?' she husked, and he knew he could lead her there if he wanted. That this time she'd welcome him.

He moved away from her.

'Dante—' She reached for him.

He shook his head. Kept moving until the distance between them felt endless.

For months, he'd thought of nothing but *her*. The feel of her against him. Her skin. Her taste. She'd haunted his every living moment. In his waking hours and his sleep.

He shut his eyes against it. The something in his chest he didn't recognise. A pain. A tug.

He didn't want it. Whatever it was. Whatever she was bringing to the surface.

'It's late,' he said.

He wanted her. But he didn't want this. This new Emma who spoke of her feelings. Her pain. This Emma who wanted to know his pain.

He wanted none of it.

So tonight he would walk away.

He'd reset. He'd find another way to show her how they maintained the balance in their marriage.

No emotions. No discussions of childhood trauma. Only them. Only sex.

'Good night, Emma.'

CHAPTER SIX

DANTE'S PLAN HAD always been flawed. He could see that now.

He'd brought Emma to Japan to thrill her. But Emma had never cared to chase the thrill of worldly adventures. She'd wanted the extravagance of *normal* many took for granted. She longed for security in the safety of his arms. A passionate marriage in the confines of a contract. But a loveless marriage.

He'd dismissed key information that he already knew about her. He understood she longed for financial security and passion without emotional attachment.

Now he understood *why*…

Emma didn't want to explore the heat between them, because she didn't trust it.

Didn't trust *him*.

But tonight, he'd prove that she could.

For three days, he'd planned, and curated a campaign of seduction that had nothing to do with shared trauma. Nothing to do with emotions or feelings. Only what would excite and delight *her* senses.

Tonight, he'd delight her. Win her trust. And then they would get this marriage back on track.

His body tightened in anticipation. He'd blocked out the intensity of his longing, his conviction to allow Emma the space she demanded. Tonight she needed to see it.

He opened his eyes and scanned his scene of seduction.

Fires burned in small ceramic pots, positioned at every corner of the square, white-clothed table set for two. A black gold-embossed menu sat prepared to be opened by her fingers and devoured by her senses as she read beneath long-stemmed candles. The menu was curated to tantalise her taste buds, to show her the man who'd written it, knew her. Her likes—*dislikes*.

He'd cater to her every worldly desire, while she dined with him in this man-made cherry blossom grove, under a night's sky.

Then he'd meet her every physical desire too.

The black double doors opened. The two doormen held them open with white-gloved hands and dipped heads.

And she stole the breath in his lungs.

She was a vision.

The dress was everything he knew it would be. Decadent. Made of silver sequins hand sewn into a delicate blood-red silk overlaid with purple-and-black lace. Her shoulders and back were bare. A tight bodice nipped in at the waist and flared out in a fishtail.

Dante watched her from the shadows. Watched the sway of her feminine curves as she walked the white stone path snaking beneath her feet.

Her eyes rose to the treetops, her heavy blond hair swishing between her shoulder blades, and he caught the glints of the sliver clasp containing her hair into a high ponytail. And his fingers itched to touch it. To release it. To watch her hair fall to her naked shoulders before he gripped it between his fingers.

But still, he didn't move.

Still, he watched.

Her gaze moved along every tree, every overarching branch that created a shelter overhead. She scanned the petals. The most vivid pinks to the purest whites.

Her eyes dipped to the flowerbeds. To the wild flowers of pink and yellow. To the orange blooms with stained red tips.

And she was iridescent, glowing beneath the soft amber glow of the lanterns hanging from the intermittent branches of every tree.

She looked like she belonged here. Some mythical creature sent to command the trees. The flowers.

Dante flinched, an imperceptible jolt of his body beneath his suit as the memory assaulted him.

The memory of a basket overflowing with delicacies, overturned. Their clothes strewn on each step towards the bedroom.

Her surprise picnic forgotten.

He'd forgotten her love of gardens that night.

Forgotten the reason they'd chosen the house in Mayfair.

Dante remembered now.

He'd picked her up from work and driven them to the viewing. But instead of going inside, he'd taken her into the garden. The secret garden. And she'd lit up. Something inside her glowing at this secret world, living and alive, within the concrete jungle of London.

So he'd taken her to every house with a secret garden and he'd bought her the first one she adored.

He hadn't been able to convince her to give up any of her three jobs initially after the move into the Mayfair house, after their engagement. None of them. Thankless jobs. A silver service waitress at night, a cafe catering assistant in the day and an agency cleaner on the side...

Somewhere inside her she'd been afraid, even then, that he wouldn't take care of her, hadn't she? That his promise of marriage was a lie until he slipped the ring on her finger and they both signed on the dotted line.

But he had taken care of her, met her needs.

Then why did she leave you?

Something heavy shifted inside him. He ignored it.

She was here *now.* That was what mattered, what he was focused on.

She had arrived at the table, stood next to it now,

fingering the candlesticks, the crystal glasses, the silverware—

Dante moved towards her now, through the trees on silent feet.

He stepped into her space behind her, and it hit him in the solar plexus. The presence of her. Her scent.

She turned, eyes wide. 'Dante!' She placed a hand to his chest, to steady herself. 'Thank you,' she said, and her eyes glittered. 'I adore *this*. Gardens…' Her eyes moved from his to the trees—to the flowers. 'Me and Mum moved around a lot, inner city estate to inner city estate. Flats to maisonettes to houses. But there was always a garden,' she said.

He felt her heavy swallow.

'Whether it was potted plants on a windowsill or a shared communal garden. I used to steal Mum's library books and sneak out in the dead of night to read them beneath the lights I'd threaded between the trees. To escape for a while. Just for a time where I could forget the hardness. Mum's tears… The garden was a safe place where all was quiet. All was still.'

His eyes travelled down over her plump parted lips. Down over her throat. Over the prominent arch of her collarbone. And he wanted to carry her back the way she'd come. Up to the suite. To bed. And lose himself in her. Silence her lips with his and end these stories of hers he didn't want to hear. Didn't *need* to hear.

But he didn't. He remained still. Let the thud of his heart beat ferociously beneath her fingertips.

'I figured it out.'

'What?'

'Our marriage,' she replied. 'It makes sense now.'

His frowned. 'What does?'

'Both our childhoods were…*unstable*. And we found stability in each other. A frantic all-consuming stability.'

He clenched his fists at his sides to stop him reaching for her. To stop him from spanning his palms around her waist to explore the dip before he came to the arch of her hips. To stop him from tugging her body into the groove of his to show her just how well their bodies fitted together. To prove to her she needed no more words. No more talk. Not whatever *this* was.

Only him.

'*You* are my garden,' she concluded, and her words shredded his resolve to be slow. To ease her into the physicality of his desire. Of hers.

He was not her…*garden*.

He had to tell her everything. *Everything*. The contract. The rules…

He couldn't allow her to speculate, to come up with her own truth.

He'd seduce with the truth she needed to hear. Why she trusted him. Why she'd married him.

He needed to end whatever fantasies she was creating about their commitment to one another.

'Our marriage has nothing to do with…gardens, Emma,' he stated. 'It has everything to do with how I make you feel. How you make me feel.'

Her eyes narrowed and moved over the hard jut of his jaw to the flickering pulse in his cheek. 'How you make me feel?'

'We have a contract.'

'A contract?'

'A purely-for-passion marriage for as long as we both see fit for it to continue. We agreed to one year originally. Planned for another three years if we were still content. Happy in the confines of our contract. And we *were* content,' he assured her, because they had been. He was sure of that. Or at least he had been.

But she left. The contract has technically expired.

Semantics. There was no need to press on the separation between them. He'd tell her the facts. Facts as he knew them. And she needed to hear them; he had no other choice but to tell her. Because he could not allow her to turn them into something else. Something he didn't want. Something that needed to be fed and watered and nourished emotionally.

He didn't want it.

And neither did she.

'There was no chance of you ever becoming your mother, Emma,' he told her, because he knew this was the way now. The only way to re-establish what they were. What he wanted again. 'Because we both wanted the same thing from our marriage. Each other. Without emotional attachments. Without love. We do not know how to love, Emma, because we understand it as the lie it is. But we trust each other. To stick to the terms in the contract,' he said, her breaths coming in quick sharp rasps.

'Terms?'

'Yes, a simple contract, to take what we wanted from each other,' he reiterated, 'Until we were sated.'

He was not sated. And he didn't believe she was either.

'What happened when we were done?' she asked. 'When it was over between us?'

'We'd divorce and you'd receive a settlement. You'd be financially secure for ever.'

'And what did you get out of this arrangement?'

'You.' Her fingers clenched and clung to his shirt. 'We can have that again, Emma,' he said roughly, his voice hoarse. 'We can—'

'Have a physical relationship—*a marriage*,' she corrected, 'without emotional attachment.' He watched the blush bloom in her pale cheeks. The flair of her nostrils. The unsteady rise and fall of her chest. 'Without lies or deception. No broken promises. Just...*sex*. Until I no longer want you.'

'Or I no longer want *you*,' he added, because if he was to have Emma in his bed again, she needed to understand the rules they played by.

'I—'

He shook his head. 'Understand this before you say anything,' he growled. 'Whether you want to stay in this marriage or not, everything I've said still stands. If you choose to leave, you will be financially secure. But if—'

'If I want you to take me to bed,' she said, 'it will

be sex only?' Her blue eyes were fixed on his, probing, searching.

'Exactly,' he agreed, and something inside him
shifted. But it didn't feel like triumph. It was not
elation zipping through his veins. It was heavier.
Darker.

'No emotions involved, Emma. Only desire. Only
want.' He placed his hand on top of hers. Watched
her mouth fall open as his fingers covered her.

'I can fulfil your every physical desire,' he promised, because he could.

He *would*.

For three days and three months, he'd waited.
Thinking of this moment. Of his Emma coming
back to him. How he'd take his power back by giving her the illusion of hers. But in this moment, he
didn't feel powerful.

He felt displaced.

Alone on the ledge.

Waiting.

For her.

It felt like whiplash.

Emma ached with everything she now knew about
their marriage and everything she still didn't. He'd
given her what she'd asked for on the terrace.

A better understanding of him.

But she wasn't satisfied.

He'd brought her to a forest of cherry blossoms,
a garden with a variety of spring blooms. Some she
knew and some she didn't. Iris. Yellow petals with

stained tips of red. Tulip Don Quichotte. Deep strains of purple and pink.

It was overwhelming he'd do this for her. A wife who was supposed to mean nothing to him. Not emotionally.

It was as if he knew her. Not only her body as per their contract. But the woman beneath all that.

He'd created a place for her in his mind.

A place filled with knowledge of her.

This wasn't sexual.

It *was* intimate. It was holding her hand, when every instinct told her to withdraw from his touch. It was knowing her in ways that had nothing to do with her body.

He saw her. He made her feel safe. And wanted.

But none of it mattered, apparently.

It had never mattered between them.

She'd exposed herself, spoken freely about her past, taken some of her power back by exposing the truth. And for what? Their marriage had only ever been surface deep. It was a connection of bodies, not minds. Not hearts.

They had a contract. No emotional attachment, no love. Only them and a shared desire. A marriage strictly for passion with an inbuilt safety net and financial security guaranteed.

And…*sex*.

Lots of sex.

Questions, so many questions, caught in her throat. Emma's throat tightened.

But it was also beginning to make sense too. How

they had found one another, why they both would have chosen to enter into a loveless marriage. They were the same, him and her. Their childhoods had both been unstable. And somehow, they'd found each other.

Each other's constant in a world that had given them both nothing but inconsistency. That was why they'd governed their relationship with rules. Put precautions in place.

'That's how you did it, isn't it?'

'Did what?'

'Convinced me to marry you.'

'Yes.'

If he'd told her about the contract the night she'd fallen, would she have stayed?

No.

The woman she'd grown into was the one who had made this possible. A woman who would have been swayed by a secure future, who wanted to be reliant on nothing and no one. One who had seen what life had to offer and what it didn't.

The younger Emma would never have risked that the intensity between them could have burned her alive. Wouldn't have risked that she might not be able to walk away. Left it behind. Left *him* behind. Because that would surely have been the easier choice.

And there was nothing wrong with choosing easy. All her life it had been hard.

Until him.

Dante had made things easier for her.

Never had she been treated softly. Never had anyone shielded her from the harshness of life. Allowed her to more than survive the endless cycle of days.

He'd come for her when she needed it the most. Taken care of her when she'd abandoned him.

Why had he done that? Was it really just about sating their desire for one another? Or had things changed over the course of their year together? Had this marriage been everything Emma had hoped for? Had she been sated? Had she had her fill of his competent mouth? His lips? His body on hers? Inside her?

She thought of the intricate lace of her underwear hidden beneath her dress. A bra. Suspenders. Stockings.

Never to her knowledge had she worn anything like it before, but she had instinctually worn them tonight. And that made her feel brave. Sensual. In a way that Emma at only twenty-two would never have been.

Ever since Dante had come to her aid in the hospital, she had felt a void in her open up. Was this the way to satisfy that void? To indulge in the very desire that she had denied herself?

The need was so desperate she could taste it.

And why should she deny herself now? She had found the source of that hunger.

In this moment, why should she worry about why she had walked away from Dante, from their marriage? About why she had returned to Birmingham? About why she hadn't demanded a divorce and cashed in on the settlement she had been promised?

Dante was right; for whatever reason she'd written that note, she hadn't fully severed the bond between them.

And neither had he.

They'd both been waiting for each other to come back.

So tonight, she wanted to be brave.

She wanted to be sensual.

She wanted to be touched by him. She wanted to let herself be consumed by the frantic heat between them. She wanted to throw herself into the intensity of his dark brown eyes and drown in them.

She wanted to do what they had set out to do in the first place: stay until she'd had her fill, until she no longer wanted him. And then she'd walk away, without a backward glance. Whenever that might be.

Dante had promised her financial security regardless of what choice she made.

And she believed him.

It felt powerful to have this choice. To choose to please herself. *And him.*

Suddenly she felt nervous. Not wanting to bite at her lower lip and smudge the perfectly applied plum lipstick, Emma nipped at the inside of her cheek. The pain was a welcome distraction.

She knew the mechanics of sex. Understood her role in the bedroom. To be a vehicle for someone else's pleasure and take what pleasure she could of her own.

But Dante was different. How he made her feel was different. She wanted to touch him in ways she'd never touched another. She wanted to be on her knees before him and bring him pleasure with her lips. Her tongue. Her mouth. She wanted him on his knees, wanted to place her calf over his shoulder and allow him to take what he wanted.

And it felt powerful to know it would be this way for them.

No one-sided pleasure, no race to the finish line and *Whoops, sorry about that*. No apologies at all.

With him, it would be mutual. A shared goal to please one another.

Dante's eyes moved over every exposed area of her skin. And it heated her from the inside.

She recognised it. The wildfire that would ignite as soon as his lips touched hers.

An ache pulsed inside her.

This time, she'd let him catch fire.

Let it roar inside her.

Let it roar inside them both.

She'd made her choice.

Tonight, she'd be with Dante without emotion. He'd fulfil her every physical desire, and she'd embrace the franticness. The intensity.

What was the harm?

Emma pushed her hand into the hard muscle of his chest. Felt the ripple of the white dress shirt beneath her fingers. Let the heat of his hand on hers warm her. Heat her from her toes to her scalp.

'Kiss me,' she demanded, and it felt powerful to demand it. To want him without fear.

'Emma,' he warned darkly. And she felt the rumble of it in his chest, beneath her hand.

'I need more than that. I need you to tell me exactly what you want, what you're choosing.'

Emma needed to say it out loud as much as he needed to hear it. That she was willing to accept his terms, the terms they had put in place together for this marriage to work.

'I choose our marriage. The contract. No emotion. Only desire. I choose…'

Slowly, she let her gaze move over his face. It was perfectly symmetrical. Black hair hung at his ears. High cheekbones sat above his powerful jaw and noble nose. And his eyes, a brown so dark, so deep, she could fall into them.

'You…' she breathed.

'Emmy…' Her name wasn't a warning. It was a plea. She recognised it, because her body pleaded with her too. Begged her to give in to the heat between them.

To surrender. Emma rose on her tiptoes and began to close the distance between them. And with every millimetre she felt the anticipation climb inside her.

Until Dante finally caught her mouth with his.

CHAPTER SEVEN

DANTE WAS DROWNING in her. Drowning in Emma's kiss.

A growl rose in him as he caressed her lips.

The confirmation that she wanted to come back to him, to where she belonged, took his breath away. He couldn't get close enough to her, to the source of sustenance his body craved.

He had fantasised about this moment for too long. The fantasy had once been his reality. The taste of her lips. Warm. Spiced. And he'd sipped from her lips, again and again, indulging in her mouth, her tongue, until all he could taste was her.

Until she was gone.

Then the fantasy had become his wildest dream. Fevered nights and days remembering her. Trying to forget her. But wanting her. And here she was now, wanting him.

He tried to get even closer. To satisfy the compulsion to get nearer.

He bowed his chest into hers. Into her breasts. Pressed his hardness into her softness.

He palmed her with his hands. Caressed her naked

shoulders. Stroked her waist as he inched his way towards her back, towards the naked dip in her spine, and pressed his fingers into her flesh. Dragged her into him.

But it wasn't enough.

So he devoured her.

He swept the crease of her mouth with his tongue until it opened for him, allowing him to taste her more deeply.

It still wasn't enough.

There was nothing between them but the thin barrier of their clothes. And what he wanted was to release her so that they could shed them, but he could not release her. Could not command his brain to do what he wanted. What he knew they both wanted.

'Emmy...' he moaned against her. And he barely recognised the visceral rawness.

His body was on fire, but his brain was whispering in tongues. His body was responding to a language he didn't speak.

Restraining him.

The shackles were invisible. But he felt them on his wrists. Holding him back.

Dante pleaded in silent prayer. He wanted to be gentle with her the first time they came together. But he felt anything but gentle. He wanted to take her here, in this garden.

But everything inside him was urging—*demanding*—he go slower. Taste every inch of the skin he had missed. Press against the heat of her and linger there, in the warmth of her.

Emma suddenly pushed him away, tearing his mouth from her.

The urge to reach for her, to keep his hold on her, was so strong.

Her eyes, wild and wide, heavy with desire, locked onto his.

And he watched, mesmerised, as she moved over to the table, took a seat, right on its edge.

He stood rooted to the spot. Aching. Watching.

'I want you. *Here…*' she breathed, and the confession halted whatever air had made it into his airways.

And still he could not move. Could not join her at the table's edge.

'Please,' she said, and his heart hammered.

If he took her here, now, that would be her memory of them.

The first memory of them coming together. He did not want that.

What do you want?

His gaze moved over her swollen lips. Proof of how strong their desire was. How strong it had always been.

And yet, it was not the same. He was not the same. She was not the same. He didn't know why. Only that it was different.

The people who had met at that charity event were not here.

Something snapped inside him.

Released him.

She deserved more. And so did he. He moved then. Claimed her chin beneath his thumb and forefinger, ignoring the rasp of her breath, the shudder she made as her bottom lip trembled.

She deserved more than quick satisfaction. More than an indecent encounter anyone could see.

'I can take you here,' he told her, and his erection pulsed. 'I can fall to my knees and taste you again. I can make you come with my mouth on you, with my fingers. I can ready you for me. I can do all those things. *More*. I can thrust inside you, right here. Right now.'

The delicate tendons in her throat constricted. 'But you won't?'

His thumb and forefinger gripped her chin more tightly. Forced her gaze to stay locked on his. Because he hated what his confession had caused her. He saw it. A flash of doubt. Of pain.

She thought he was rejecting her.

'Do not,' he growled, 'doubt how much I want this.' He released her chin and sought her hand. Claimed it and brought it between them. Placed her open palm on the part of him that ached for her.

'Do not doubt,' he said again, the hardness of him pulsing beneath her fingers, 'how much I want you, Emmy.' Her eyes blazed. 'I want you in every way imaginable. To be inside you…'

He closed his eyes because it was painful to resist. A deep hurt was growing inside him with his every word that opposed his frantic desire.

'Then why won't you?' she asked, her fingers on him. Tentatively she stroked him.

He opened his eyes. 'We deserve a bed,' he breathed raggedly.

He knew what he wanted now. Her in his bed. To savour her. To keep her there between the sheets where she couldn't escape. Wouldn't want to leave. Today. Tomorrow. Or ever.

'A bed?'

'I would prefer our bed in Mayfair,' he said, his abdomen flexing at the flash of an empty bed. Their bed. Abandoned by her.

'But we would never make it that long.'

His confession caused him to tremble at the effort it took to restrain himself. The effort of not doing what she'd asked him to do and take her. Here.

But he would not.

'You're shaking,' she gasped.

'As you will be,' he promised. 'If you let me take you to bed. I will make you come so hard your knees will shake. *Uncontrollably*. And then I will do it again, and again, until all you know, all you understand, is this. The need pulsing between us. A need that never dies. That always wants more.'

He was rigid with it now. Painful desire, and something else. Something he couldn't place.

The day he'd readied their new contract, three more years to explore the depths of their desire, he'd felt a contentment. An easiness he'd never had. Because for once, he'd not felt the urge for more, as Cappetta men always did. To climb higher peaks, or to parachute over more perilous terrains. His only urge was simply to keep her.

He felt that now, alongside his desire. Contentment.

He wasn't so naive. This obsession with her, his little crush, would end. *Eventually*. And then and only then would he end it.

But not yet.

'Will you let me take you to bed?' he asked, because that was what he needed. A bed and her in it.

There was nothing else to want. Nothing else *he* needed. Only her flesh. Only her body. Only sex.

'There will be no need to rush. No need to be quick. And I won't be quick, Emmy,' he promised. A promise he'd keep like all the others he'd made to her. 'I will take my time with you. Savour you.'

'Savour me?' she asked, her lips parting on a mew.

It fed him.

Revived him.

His neck stiff with tension, he nodded his confirmation.

'Slowly,' he promised. 'I will savour every inch of you.'

He leaned down until his mouth hovered above the soft flesh beneath her ear and whispered, 'Will you come with me, Emmy?'

He pulled back just enough to watch as her blue eyes sought his and he let her hold them captive. Let her search their depths. Because he knew what she would see. Only the heat between them.

Tentatively, her fingers rose to his waist, travelled farther up, with feather-light precision. With splayed fingers and open palm, her hand sat on his chest.

Just like it had been at the beginning of them.

Then, slowly, she moved her hand from his chest and reached for his hand. And claimed it.

'I'll come with you.'

When he looked down at their hands, he saw their gold wedding bands glistening. Reminding him of the promises they'd shared with one another. The rules they'd vowed to obey.

She trusted him to take her back there. Back to the marriage they'd had before. Could still have by following the rules they had created.

Because without the rules there was no them.

His fingers tightened around hers.

'Come,' he rasped, and tugged her down the white stone path, back through the double doors.

Soon, so very soon, their clothes would be strewn on every surface, and they would at last be in bed, together. And they would stay there. Stay there until his obsession died.

With every step across the marbled foyer of the Cappetta hotel, Emma's skin tingled with anticipation. It spread up from her toes, up the backs of her calves, up the muscles in her thighs and pooled at the intimate heart of her.

Then it radiated out in waves.

Neither had spoken. But still he held her hand. Still, she held his.

Even as they entered the private lift to their suite, even as the steel doors closed.

Side by side, they stood, and the silence pulsed.

Never had a man shaken with desire for her. Never had a man wanted to…

Savour her.

Slowly.

But Dante had done, wanted to do, both of those things.

And it spoke to her. To the secret parts inside her that longed for those things. To be savoured. To be precious to someone. Protected because someone cared.

And he cared, didn't he?

The realisation was acute. It was a piercing pain in her chest. Because all the things her mother had been waiting for her father to provide, Emma had. With Dante.

He was taking care of her, had taken care of her, in all the ways she hadn't been able to take care of herself. Hadn't seen herself as worthy of. Or allowed herself to want them. Because belief and hope, they were dangerous. Deadly.

She closed her eyes. Shut everything out. Because all her life she'd been running from her feelings, her needs, her secret desires. Afraid she'd turn out like her mum. Unloved and unwanted. But Emma *was* wanted. Not loved. But she was cared for. Protected.

And it was enough.

It was what she wanted.

Slowly, she opened her eyes, turned her head and looked up at him from behind lowered lashes.

So why had she left when she had it so good?

Did it matter anymore?

Higher and higher the lift climbed, until it announced its arrival at the top floor.

Dante turned, the invitation in his gaze mirroring her own.

'We deserve a bed,' she said, because he was right. They deserved to explore, to rediscover, their marriage with care. With softness. With consideration.

'We do,' he agreed roughly.

Emma moved her gaze to the lift doors. Eyed her reflection in the steel. Stared at her body. A body he knew intimately.

She wondered if he would cradle her breasts as softly as he'd cradled her face in the hospital? Would he slowly apply pressure as she moaned into his mouth? Would she tell him what she liked? That she wanted her nipple in his mouth and that she wanted him to suck? To bite? Would he caress the swell of her stomach? Would his hand move slowly or urgently to the dark hairs curling between her legs?

She wanted to know all these things. How he would touch her. How his touch would be different.

The steel doors opened to their suite.

'Ready?' he asked roughly.

Was she? Was she ready to not only survive the night, but to *own* it.

'I'm ready.'

CHAPTER EIGHT

TOGETHER, EMMA AND Dante moved through the penthouse suite with haste. So quickly that she barely acknowledged how magnificent it was. A mansion all on one level. Made of black marble with silver edges and glass. Huge vases held small cherry blossom trees, pink petals falling everywhere.

As they reached the bedroom door, he slowed.

The fingers in hers loosened and were pulled from her grasp.

Dante opened the door, and stepped aside to allow her to enter. Her gaze moved to the floor-to-ceiling windows that formed two of the four walls of the room.

Outside she could see the bright lights on the city—gold and white and red.

How many rooms like this had she stood in with Dante? How many stories had they shared in rooms she couldn't remember? How many beds had they found each other in until he had demanded they have just the one bed?

Before he had proposed they marry?

Did it matter? Tonight, *this* would be their bed. The only bed she'd remember sharing with him.

Her eyes moved to the white stone wall to her left, over the soft lights glowing like candles, down to the black wooden headboard carved with swirls, to the bed. An imposing bed of stark white pillows and black sheets.

Excitement pulsed through her in a tidal wave of heat.

She stepped towards the bed—

'Wait.' Strong fingers locked around her wrist. His large masculine hand commanded she be still.

'I don't want to wait,' she said, her skin tingling, her body demanding she find release from this tension holding her every limb hostage.

His thumb stroked the pulse point on her wrist. 'I want to undress you.' He released her wrist. Breath hit her nape, a whisper of warmth on her skin, and the pulse in her core quickened. *'Slowly.'*

He pressed in behind her, and her spine arched into him. The outline of his body penetrated hers, the heat of him seeping inside every pore of her exposed flesh.

Never had she been undressed with care when urgency demanded they were already naked.

It was dizzying.

'Then undress me,' she demanded, her voice smoky. And it felt like she was giving him more than the permission to remove her clothes. But to remove her armour too. Because never had anyone unwrapped her like a gift. Like she was something *special*. Or maybe Dante had, but she just couldn't remember.

'I will. But first I want to do this.' *Click*. Her hair fell from its high ponytail to fall to her shoulders.

His fingers speared into her hair, loosening the strands. 'I have dreamed of your hair. Feeling it through my fingers. Wrapped around my fist.'

Her heart hiccupped. 'You've dreamed of me?'

'Yes.' He swept her hair over her left shoulder, over her taut collarbone. And the touch was teasing. It was too light. Not what she wanted. She wanted his hands. She wanted his touch to imprint itself on her, to brand her.

When his knuckle grazed down her naked spine, she couldn't hold it in. The gasp.

'Every night—' the whisper of his lips grazed her nape '—I have thought of nothing but kissing you here.' Feather-light, he placed his mouth to the tip of her spine. 'And here.'

His lips lifted from her skin to move to the flesh of her throat. Where her neck met her shoulder. And a noise was ripped from her lips. A wail that demanded he give her more.

His mouth climbed higher, a teasing caress of his mouth, to the spot behind her ear, and Dante whispered, 'And here.'

And the lips that had fluttered gently across her skin now pressed deeper. Sank deeper into her flesh. He pulled the skin between them and sucked.

Until Emma panted. Until she was breathless with the sensations his mouth tugged from her core.

His fingers pressed into the dip of her spine and she gasped as he tugged the zip down her buttocks to the top of her thighs.

His hands spanned her waist as he brought her back into him, his arousal pressed into her bottom.

'*Please...*' Emma could barely stand it any longer.

'Turn around,' he commanded, and on unsteady feet, she did.

Her breath hitched as black eyes caught hers.

'Please what, Emmy?'

'More,' she confessed. 'I want *more*.'

'More of what?' he asked. 'My hands?' His hands moved back to her waist and up. 'My fingers?' His fingertips brushed the sensitive flesh beneath her arms.

Dante peeled the bodice of her dress down over her breasts, revealing the sheer black lace of her bra. And her nipples strained against it.

'My mouth?'

'Yes,' she replied, 'I want them all.'

His hands cupped her breasts.

'Like this?'

She swallowed. 'Harder.'

His fingers held her firmly, his thumbs flicking over the pebbled peaks. 'Better?'

'Yes.'

'And now, do you want my mouth?'

'Please,' she mewed. 'Yes, please.'

His head dipped to her breast, and he sucked her nipple into his mouth until it throbbed. *Pulsed.*

He lifted his mouth—

'No!' Her hands reached for him. Clung to the lapels of his black dinner jacket.

'No more?' he asked, nostrils flaring.

'No,' she corrected, her voice not her own. It was wanton. '*Please*, don't stop.'

With deft fingers, he released the front clasp of her bra and let it drop to the floor.

His eyes coveted her chest. 'You have beautiful breasts,' he said.

She cried out as he dipped his head again, took the neglected breast into his mouth and suckled.

The blood in her veins whooshed deafeningly with the speed of her heart.

He tugged at the skirt of her dress, pulling it down. But this time his lips remained on her skin. His kiss moved down the valley between her breasts. To the flat of her stomach. And her skirt went down with him. Past her thighs, her knees. Until it fell to the floor and pooled at her feet and she stepped out of it. And Dante was on his knees before her.

'For months,' he growled, his features tight, dark, 'I have thought of the taste of you. Your skin. How it trembles beneath my mouth. How it sings for me. For my touch.'

Her pulse slowed. She searched his gaze, watched as it burned with something primal. Possessive. 'Only my touch.'

The possessive sentiment didn't scare her anymore. It made her burn. Made her wet between her legs. It excited her.

His hands gently parted her thighs, and she opened

them for him. 'Can you feel it, Emma?' he asked. 'The adrenaline building between us?' His thumbs stroked her on the inner flesh of her thighs. 'The power of it?'

Heart raging, she nodded.

'Put your left hand on my shoulder,' he demanded, and she did. She reached for him. Held on to the tight hard muscle of him and steadied herself.

Anticipation thrummed through her. Quickened her pulse. Her breathing. Every nerve ending was exposed.

His eyes holding hers, his hand stroked down her right inner thigh, to graze along her knee, until he gripped her sheer-black-stocking-covered calf and lifted it. Placed it on his shoulder.

He stroked back the way he came. Back up to her knee with a gentle drag of his fingers, up her thigh, until he stroked her. There.

'Do you want my mouth here?' he asked, his voice a dark thing. A hot thing that spoke directly to her sex. And it pulsed. Clenched in places she couldn't name. Couldn't decipher. But she wanted that. His intimate kiss.

'Please...' she breathed. 'Kiss me. Kiss me now.'

A guttural noise from deep in his chest vibrated in her ears. On her skin. And then his mouth was there again. Kissing her on top of the fabric. His tongue slowly sliding against her intimate folds.

Emma reached for his head and pushed her fingers into the raven silk of his hair and pulled his mouth closer to her core. The faster he moved his tongue, the deeper he licked, the ache inside her sharpened, tightened.

'Oh… Oh. *Oh!*' she gasped, again, and again, as he speared his tongue between her sex, until his lips claimed the pulsing nub at the apex of her sex and sucked.

Faster and faster, until she couldn't catch her breath. Couldn't breathe for the sensations rippling through her body. Sensations of unlimited pleasure and relentless passion that he was gifting her.

And the need for more was overwhelming. And it was demanding. Demanding that she chase it. This feeling. This rush.

Her hands moved everywhere. Over his scalp. His shoulders. Pulling him nearer to her.

With his hands on her hips, he held her steady against his mouth. Let her body rock against his mouth.

And then he released her and his hand went between her thighs, pulled aside her panties and claimed her oversensitive nub without the hindrance of the lace. The pleasure was almost unbearable.

She threw her neck back involuntarily.

Two fingers entered her. Stretched her. Until they slipped in to the hilt, and pumped.

'Oh, my God!' Tightly, she held on to him, relying on the support of his shoulders. His hand on her hip. She was going to fall. She was—

'Coming,' she breathed. 'I'm—'

A third finger pushed inside her.

'Oh!' She was full, so full of him. But her body

wanted more. It wanted the thick length of him where she ached the most.

'I want you inside me,' she admitted.

'Soon,' he breathed. 'I want to pleasure you first.'

Her thoughts became disjointed, disoriented.

'I want you wet,' he rasped. 'I want you ready to take me. All of me inside you,' he rasped, and his words fired her blood into a hot, raging, needy thing that needed more. More oxygen. More water. More of something that she couldn't identify. But most of all it needed him.

His fingers curled inside her. Found a place she didn't know lived inside her and pushed against it. Stroked it. Until all she could feel was pleasure.

Emma fought her release. It felt too big, both in this moment and the journey that she had been on to chase it. She knew that what was coming, what was building inside her, had the ability to break her, to shatter her, to change her completely.

And it was everything he'd promised it would be. A rush. A high she'd never found with anyone but him.

'Come for me,' he roared against her skin, her flesh singing for him.

He wanted this. *Her*. Undone in ways she could never have imagined in her wildest dreams. And she wanted it too. To strip herself of the chains she'd shackled herself with and surrender to it. To what they were. To who *she* was with him. Bold. Sensual. Fearless in his arms.

She truly understood now why she had chosen

Dante. For the first time since her accident she was confident that this was where she was meant to be. Where she was always meant to be. In Dante's arms. In his bed. In this marriage they'd created to suit each other. She was safe to expose all her needs. All her physical wants. Without consequence.

Only then did she let go.

Without fear.

Without inhibition.

'Dante!' she screamed. Every syllable was torn from somewhere deep inside her…

Carefully, Dante withdrew from Emma before standing and reaching for her again. Pulling her into his embrace and lifting her into his arms.

'Dante—'

'Shush,' he breathed. Quietly, although nothing within him was quiet.

His body demanded more than her undoing. It not only demanded everything they'd had before, but it demanded… He wasn't quite sure. But he knew her being back in his arms didn't feel like enough. His gut told him so.

And yet he didn't trust it. His instinct was to fasten his mouth to hers and take them to bed and ignore that feeling. To find oblivion in the two of them coming together.

Never in his life had performance anxiety made him falter. But he was faltering now. Denying himself his primal needs because he was thinking about what came afterwards.

That concept was alien to him, though. He didn't quite know what to do with it. And so he'd do nothing; he'd stay firmly in this moment and he'd take his time. Prolong the moment until he would have to face that foreign feeling again.

His neck dipped, and he met her gaze.

'Thank you,' she said, and her fingers splayed on his heated cheek. 'That was—'

'Only the beginning,' he said, because he did not want her thanks. He wanted his wife back.

And she *was* coming back to him. It was all that mattered. Having her beneath him, where she belonged and where she'd stay until his body no longer ached.

He swept her into his arms and carried her over to the bed. And she clung onto him, her arms around his neck, breathing against it, her breath fanning across his flesh.

'I will make this good for you,' he promised rawly.

'I know,' she said. She trusted him to keep his word. To meet her every desire.

And he would.

He'd make her shake. Tremble. With a desire so rampant, so addictive, that neither would be able to think straight.

She reached for him as he set her on the edge of the bed, placing a hand on his stomach.

'I want to learn every inch of you,' she confessed, her fingers moving to the silver buckle of his belt. 'I want to learn how to give you pleasure too.' A blush bloomed a deep scarlet on her cheeks. But she did not release his eyes. She did not remove her hand. 'I want to pleasure you with my mouth.'

He nodded. A single dip of his head, because he didn't trust himself to speak. Because he had only missed her body, her mouth, not *her*.

Slowly, she unbuckled him. And he made himself stand still. Taut. As he prepared himself for the silkiness of her mouth. The warmth.

Belt open, she undid his button, splayed the waistband of his trousers, and her hand crept inside his boxers. She withdrew him with gentle fingers. Until he was free and his arousal stood tall and erect in her small, pale hand.

Her blond head dipped…

'Emma,' he said, and she flicked her tongue over the tip of him, the silken edge beading with his need for her to take him deeper.

And she took him, inch by inch, until her throat flexed and accept him, and he—

'Emma!' he roared as she sucked him. Used her pale hand to pump him in unison with the slide of her lips, the sheath of her warm, wet mouth.

He fisted her hair. Wrapped it around the palm of his hand. Watched her please him.

And he couldn't stand it. How easily she took him to the edge of his control. How easily she undid him. How easily she made a mockery of the way in which he ran his life, the rules he'd put in place.

'Emma, stop,' he growled, need lacing the words. Because she would not undo him yet. He wouldn't lose control. He would show her the strength of his control. The power he had over himself to resist the ultimate satisfaction so that he could bring them both to climax, together.

He drew an agonising breath into tight lungs. 'Can you feel what you do to me?' he asked breathlessly. 'I'm so hard, it hurts, Emmy. But I don't want to spill myself into your mouth. I want to be *inside* you. To feel you wrapped around me as I drive you to the edge again,' he said. 'I *need* to be inside you,' he confessed.

'I want that too,' she breathed, and with gritted teeth, he watched her slither back into the centre of the bed.

'Come to bed,' she breathed. It was all he'd wanted for months. To hear his wife say those words.

He reached for the tie at his throat. Loosened it, tugged it free, and let it flutter to the floor. The buttons were next. So many of them that it felt like an eternity before he could bare himself.

Her gaze seared his skin. But he didn't stop. He removed his trousers, his boxers, socks and shoes.

He crawled between her thighs. Felt her raise her hips to meet him, meet the hardness of him pulsing against her. And he removed the final barrier between them, the black lace of her panties. Pulling them down over her calves, her ankles, and tossing them aside.

On the way back, he kissed the exposed softness of her ankle bone, her knee, her inner thigh.

'Put your legs on my shoulders,' he commanded, because he wanted her open to him. For her to be in a position to take all of him so deeply she wouldn't be able to breathe for the fullness.

She did as he instructed, and he shifted against her, feeling how ready she was for him, the wetness at her core.

His need to be inside her was frantic, all consuming.

And he pressed into the intimate centre of her, entered her. Slowly, inch by inch.

He took his time, knowing that once he was fully inside her he would be lost to the urgency between them. Compelled by the need to drive into her again and again until his body was released from the hold she had over him.

He needed a moment to gain back a modicum of control.

'Dante, do you want to…stop?'

'Is that what you want?' he growled, his neck straining as he fought every instinct to thrust up inside her.

'No.' Her hair, strewn over the white pillow, moved with the shake of her head. And he wanted to fist it. Drag her mouth to his.

'I want to go slow,' he admitted. 'I don't want to hurt you.'

'You won't hurt me,' she promised. 'My body will remember you.'

Her hips flexed, and she took him inside her a little more. 'But if you want to stop,' she said, and he heard the tightness in her voice. Heard a need he mirrored in his taut muscles, begging for release. 'We can.'

'I do not want that,' he ground out.

Her hands, open palmed, smoothed over his chest. And when she ran her fingertips over his bruised nipples, her touch ignited a fire in his skin. And he was burning.

'Then don't stop.'

Sweat beaded on his brow. 'I won't.'

He thrust up into her.

'Yes!' Her face contorted. 'Again. *More*.'

He gripped her hips, plunged, hard and deep.

Dante strained against his instincts, despite her words, despite his, to do what he wanted and take her mindlessly.

His muscles burned with his resistance. If he did these things, if he let go, gave in to the animalistic instinct to rut these thoughts away, he'd hurt her.

Slowly, he slid into her again and again, let her body remember him. Welcome him back.

Her ankles locked around his neck. 'Faster, Dante,' she pleaded. *'Harder.'*

And her whispered words were what his body longed for. Had longed for, for months. And she knew, didn't she? She knew what he needed because she needed it too. To end the endless days of foreplay, the months of self-denial. To surrender to this agony between them.

'Dante, *please*!'

And whatever control he'd held on to shattered.

He possessed her.

Her body.

He came back to the only home he'd ever know, ever needed. And the truth of that overwhelmed him now.

Emma was his *home*.

And that was terrifying. But he pushed it aside.

'Never stop,' she said, and he wanted to roar.

'Dante!' Her nails bit into his skin. Into his hands. She contracted around the pulsing hardness of him, with the sweetest, most delicious vise grip.

He panted, his breath coming out in short, sharp rasps. But he did not close his eyes. Neither did she.

In sync, their hips locked. Their bodies tightened. And he no longer knew where she ended and he began.

'Emma!' he shouted as he came. Harder than he'd ever come.

And the pleasure blinded him to everything but the feel of her beneath him.

Panting, he collapsed on to his elbows and buried his face in her throat.

'That was incredible.'

'*You* are incredible,' he husked into her throat— her skin. Because she was something mystical. A creature who had crept into his life and bewitched him.

'Thank you,' she said, her hands sweeping up his back and wrapping around him.

And he was no longer blind. He could see with an undiluted clarity.

He'd won.

Emma was back.

And he'd keep her here.

Beneath him.

Where she belonged.

For now.

CHAPTER NINE

HIS CHEST ROSE beneath her cheek. His breath was rhythmic and his heart thrummed steady and strong in her ear. His arm was possessively curled around her, his hand locked to her hip. Emma couldn't move even if she wanted to. One hand on his stomach and one by her side, she stayed exactly where she was.

She'd never spent the night in anyone's bed. Never shared one for longer than she had to in her existing memory. She'd certainly never fallen asleep. But she'd slept all night with him in a tangle of limbs.

The sun streamed through the windows, highlighting the contours on his chest. Golden undertones chased by dark shadows of hair between deep lines on his abdomen led down towards the duvet that covered the lower half of his body.

Warmth gathered in the pit of her stomach. Last night had been...*a lot*.

It hadn't been perfunctory or stolen. It had been transcendent, powerful, addictive. Because even now, though her body ached, she wanted more. More of him on her. More of her on him.

She could do it *now*. Slide down his body, under

the duvet, and take him in her mouth. Wake him like that.

She could do what she liked. Take and give as much as she desired, and he'd meet her stroke for stroke as he had last night. And she'd meet him too. Kiss for kiss. Thrust for thrust. A mutual consideration of each other's pleasure.

It was *safe* sex. Emotionally and physically, she was—

Panic flared in her ribcage.

They hadn't used protection. She hadn't thought, hadn't—

Her hand shot to the flat of her stomach.

What would it mean if she was pregnant? Did they have a clause in their contract? Would that void it? She didn't want children. Did *he*? Eventually? When he married someone without a contract? When he found—

Her stomach churned.

He didn't believe in love. He said he didn't want it, that he understood, as she did, it was a lie.

'What's wrong?' He must have sensed her anxiety. Woken to it. Or perhaps she'd alerted him to her panic by tightening her grip on his stomach.

She froze. Stayed where she was on his chest. Her hand splayed taut on his abdomen.

'We didn't use protection,' she said, and listened. But the tempo of his heart remained unchanged. It was calm. Steady. 'I might be pregnant.' *Nothing.* 'I don't know when my last cycle was. I've never been consistent. I've never not used a condom. We—*I*—could get emergency contraception.'

Idly, his fingers stroked her hip bone. 'You can't be pregnant, Emma.'

'How can you be so sure?' she asked.

'I can't have children,' he said flatly as his other hand moved to her hair and smoothed over it. Over her scalp. 'I had a vasectomy many years ago. Before we met.'

A feeling settled in her chest, something heavy. And she couldn't distinguish it from relief or sorrow. It felt very similar to the blow she'd felt when Dante had told her of the loss of her mother. But that was stupid, wasn't it? To mourn the fact she'd never carry his child?

'Do you regret it?' she asked and immediately felt that she should apologise. 'I'm sorry. I shouldn't—'

'No, I don't regret it,' he answered matter-of-factly. 'I never wanted children.'

'Why not?' she asked, curiosity blooming where it shouldn't.

His heartbeat quickened.

'My mother used me as leverage against my father. He wanted an heir, and she sold him one. I never wanted to be in a similar position. Where my child was used as a bargaining chip.'

Emma jolted into a sitting position, dislodging his hands, and stared at him. 'Your mother *sold* you?'

'She did.' He remained where he was against the pillows. And he seemed almost relaxed, comfortable.

But how could that be the case when he had told her something so abhorrent?

'For how much?' she spat. 'Her soul?'

He shrugged. 'Lifetime financial security and a private island the size of a small country.'

'She—'

His eyes flashed. 'Is unimportant,' he remarked, obviously eager to be done with this line of enquiry. But Emma was not done.

'How can she be? She—'

'Has no bearing on my life.'

'You made the choice not to have children because of her.'

'And I would make that choice again.'

'How can you be so calm?'

Dante shrugged. And Emma immediately understood.

'Because you thought there was no other choice,' she said simply.

Her heart ached for him. For the little boy who had been sold and abandoned by his own mother. And she wanted to cry for him. For the man who chose to never risk a child of his being used as collateral.

She'd never wanted them either. *Children.* Never wanted to raise a child on her own. Never wanted to raise a child to *be* alone. Teach her—*him*—it was safer that way.

You aren't alone anymore.

He scowled. 'I made the choice to protect all parties involved.'

Emma became conscious of her own nakedness then. Aware of how intimate this conversation felt.

'Do not worry about the choices of the man you never knew,' he said, inching closer. 'He was eighteen. He'd just lost his father. It was the right choice to make. He—*I*—would make it again.'

His hands caught her face, then cradled her cheeks as he made her meet his eyes. 'Besides, it is a gift to be inside you without risk or consequence.'

His light-hearted tone was forced, she could tell. But she also knew that this discussion was over. And just as quickly her uncertainty was replaced by need. Unable to resist, aching for him, she kissed him.

She wanted him to pulse inside her as he had last night. She wanted him to fill her with his hardness, to push her over the edge of desire once again.

She climbed onto his lap. Slid her thighs down the bareness of his. Felt his arousal find the heart of her and tease at her entrance. She rode him, stroking herself against him.

'Emma,' he moaned against her lips. And she let it feed her newfound confidence in her sensuality. A sensuality he'd brought to the surface.

And it felt good to be bold. To be brave. To take this pleasure for herself simply because she wanted it. Wanted *him*.

'Lie back,' she said as she gently guided him back into the pillows.

And then her hands were seeking his, linking and entwining them, raising them above his head and holding them there.

The tips of her breasts were teasing against his chest. She tore her mouth from his and rose above him. Taking control, exerting her power over him.

Slowly, she took the tip of him inside her, before sinking down and taking him all. Taking him deep.

Her head fell back, her mouth opened and a moan was wrenched from her. A sound she'd never heard her body emit. It was a roar. A screech. A plea.

Emma knew all she could do was trust in their connection and surrender to it. To this urge to follow her instincts and embrace it all. The connection of their minds, their bodies. For as long as it was there.

'Ah!' He raised his hips as his hands pulled her down onto him. And it was too deep. Not deep enough.

'Dante…'

'I want to pour myself inside you,' he growled. 'I want to fill you while you pulse around me. I want to feel you tighten. Squeeze me. Until there is nothing left for me to give you.'

She lifted her hips and pushed back down. Again and again, she took him deeper than she thought her body would allow.

His breath hissed from his mouth, encouraging her to ride him faster. Take him deeper.

And Emma rode him faster.

Took him deeper.

'I'm coming,' she said, and this time she didn't resist it. She leaned into it.

She didn't have to close her eyes. She didn't have to hide who she was because he knew who she was.

She was his wife. He knew her body. What she liked. This was not a one-night stand to receive a perfunctory release.

He knew *her*. And she wanted to know him too. To give him pleasure. To receive her own. From his lips. From his body. On her. In her.

'Emmy!' he shouted, and filled her. Poured himself inside her. And she was lost in the contractions of her body. To his thickness. To his heat.

Emma lost herself to her husband.

Dante's plan had worked.

His wife was in his bed.

For almost twenty-four hours, she'd given herself to him. And he'd taken everything she was willing to let him have. They'd played out every single one of his fantasies.

He closed his eyes. Stilled the fingers stroking down her spine. Closed his eyes to the blond hair fanned out across his chest. Shut out the warmth of her body against his. Her sated, exhausted body.

He'd done that to her. Fatigued her. Pleasured her until the pleasure had seemed endless. Until she'd begged him to never stop.

He should be elated.

He should be content.

But there was no ignoring it. No ignoring that their connection had widened, deepened. That this thing between them, far from being sated, was more powerful.

It just wouldn't *die*.

And he could take her again, wake her with his kiss and accept his welcome into her body. Drive his need for her out of his body and into hers.

But it would reignite again, he knew. And continue to reignite over and over again.

She asked far too many questions, made him think far too much. Made him forget every rule he'd ever made to keep himself at a distance.

He was trying his best to remember the rules. But she kept forgetting.

And every time she forgot them, every time she asked a question he did not want to hear or think of, he'd remind her what they were. That there was no more, there was no promise of forever, of happily-ever-after. But she persisted. Would not be distracted by sex any longer.

How could he make her understand?

He wanted to be alone. He needed to be away from the bed. Away from her.

The garden flashed in his mind, along with her story of fairy lights and reading books under trees. Where all was still. All was quiet. All was safe from a world that was too loud.

He had a similar place, didn't he? No flowers, or fairy lights, but a room. A similar place in every country, every city. Somewhere he could go when he needed peace, needed quiet.

He was not so selfish, was he? To leave her behind after…

And yet, perhaps, this was how he could make her understand his need to keep people at a distance.

That for him, emotional connection wasn't something to be embraced but was to be avoided.

So he'd take her with him. To the place in Shinjuku City that he went to when he needed to centre himself, to be alone. He would show her that he wasn't a stranger to keeping himself distanced.

He swallowed thickly.

He resisted the urge to kiss her. To wake her, as he had too many times to count. Instead, he stroked her. Her hair. Her spine. Her cheek.

'Emma, wake up.'

She stirred beneath his fingers. Her bare back arching into his touch.

She pushed the hair from her eyes. 'I'm awake,' she said, and ran her open palm down his torso.

His pulse accelerated.

Lust coiled in his gut, giving life to what always lived beneath his skin. His readiness for her. To possess her.

He caught her wrist—pulled her fingers away and brought her knuckles to his mouth, brushed them against his lips.

He could be tender, couldn't he? Considerate? He was not—

He swallowed down whatever was in his throat, because he didn't want to taste it. His voice uneven, he finally spoke.

'I want to take you somewhere.'

CHAPTER TEN

IN THE BACK of the luxury car with cream leather and silver accents, they sat side by side. And together, they watched out of black windows as the car travelled through Japan's city of twinkling lights and soaring skyscrapers, until it swept through softly lit sleeping streets.

Dante swept his gaze over the profile of her. The way her fringe covered her forehead, the flick of her golden lashes, the slope of her elegant nose and the pink pout of her mouth.

Her eyes were latched on to the floating scenery, but he watched her. Watched the blue depth of her gaze that said so much, too much, when her mouth spoke words. Told him things he hadn't asked to hear and asked questions that compelled him to answer, leading to more questions.

Dante pressed his lips into a thin line and locked his jaw. He did not want to speak. He did not want to hear. He wanted to be still. *Alone.*

While Dante had travelled the world alone, he'd never taken her with him. He'd lived his life, and she'd lived hers. An arrangement that had suited them both.

Until it didn't.

Until he'd travelled across half the globe to return to their house to find her in the bed they shared, only to find that she wasn't there.

But she was here now.

The warm beige coat with a flicked-up collar hiding the bruises his mouth had created on her throat. Marking her.

He wanted to see it. His brand on her flesh.

He swallowed, drew his gaze down the loose white shirt, the thighs of her jean-clad legs, and down to the flesh-coloured heels on her feet.

His lust was hot and constant. It remained even when he didn't summon it. Even when he tried to bury it.

Throughout their marriage, he'd given her everything he'd thought she'd wanted. Exclusivity to him and his world. His billions to do with as she pleased. His body. But never his thoughts. Never his...*trauma*.

And he hadn't wanted access to hers either.

He'd never wanted her explanations of why she spent so much time in the garden. Why she was happy for their marriage to be governed by a contract.

But now he knew, and he could not unknow these stories she'd told him of her need to find a place of security and safety. To retreat from the world outside.

She'd called him her garden, and his instincts had

told him to slam down his defences and guard against her confession. But he *was* her garden, wasn't he? Not in a romanticised way. But he was her security. He was her safety. In his arms, she was safe.

And understanding why she needed that from him, needed it from their marriage, weighed heavily on him. It was precious the trust she had placed in him. Fragile. To tell him this when she didn't remember the last few years of her life, didn't remember him.

He didn't know how to hold space for such a delicate thing. How not to drop it. How not to break it, to break her. He did not want to break her.

The car halted beneath a blinking street light.

Dante scanned the street and realised they had arrived. It was an ordinary-looking place. With ordinary people walking past it towards their destination. Others stood still, talking under artificial light, and laughing. Some in groups. Some in pairs. Some holding hands.

Soft warmth infiltrated his fingers. He turned to look at the source and saw Emma's hand covering his own lying on the seat between them.

And he saw the gold ring he'd given her. That marked her as his for the world to see. At least until one of them decided they no longer wanted to be married.

He didn't like that thought, he realised. It made his nostrils flare with disgust.

He liked his ring on her finger. He liked that she was his. That she belonged to him. Because she did. And he liked that she was here. With him. Wearing her ring in this place he'd never shared with anyone else. It felt warm to have her with him. It felt…

Right.

No, that couldn't be it, could it?

'Are we getting out?' Her voice slid into his ear.

He was not so naive. He was still obsessed with her. His crush. His wife.

More obsessed than he'd ever had been, because now he wanted the thoughts in her head. Wanted her to ask questions, wanted to answer them. Despite the rules. The playbook.

Maybe they could write their own playbook. Get to know one another outside of the sex. Not love, never love. But introduce emotions.

Because her desire for stability, normality, did things to him, didn't it? Those were things he didn't know how to define or if he liked them. It was different. She was different. And she made him feel…

different.

Was she right?

Had he married her for the normality it offered, a normal he'd never truly known? Stability, sameness, one woman in his bed, in a house they shared—was that why he'd missed her? Been so displaced without her? Was this pain inside him more than a sexual ache? More than a need to possess her physically? But to…

What?

He was not normal. He wasn't raised to be normal. He could never be those things for her. And she deserved them, didn't she? This normal life she craved.

A man she came home to, who was her constant. He wasn't *that* man.

Then why are you still here?

'Dante?' His eyes met her questioning ones.

'Yes, we're getting out,' he said, and removed his hand from beneath hers as he stepped out of the car, resisting the urge to recapture it and hold it tight.

He didn't know why he was holding his breath. Why he waited with his lungs burning for her to follow him. But he did. He waited on the pavement of this ordinary street for her to join him.

'In there,' he said, and nodded towards the two black double doors to her right.

She looked at the doors. No sign to indicate what lay on the other side. To indicate if she was allowed inside. But she moved towards them and pushed one open without hesitation.

Perhaps the threat had never been outside the doors of their Mayfair house. Perhaps he was the threat. She had trusted him to keep her safe and he'd hurt her, hadn't he? By not considering what it meant to Emma when he left her behind.

Door ajar, one pointed heel inside the door, she waited for him. 'Are you coming?'

His body answered for him. A tightening in his solar plexus. Because still it lived inside him. The overwhelming need to be close to her, to be near her, to keep her close to him.

He could adapt, he knew. He could change the rules. He could show her that he hadn't listened to her stories with complete emotional detachment. But did he want to? That was the question.

Dante followed her into a place that he had thought to be his alone. A place he didn't think she belonged. He'd brought her halfway around the world to be here with him. And he could have taken her anywhere. He'd planned to seduce her with adventure and newness.

He could have taken her into Shinjuku City, dazzled her with the noise, the bustle, the lights, the smells unique to the little alley that was so big in atmosphere and its exotic food offerings, it rivalled London's Soho.

But he'd chosen to bring her here, to a place he didn't share with anyone. Not with clients. Not with anyone. It was *his*. It was not a garden. It was not a romantic place of pink petals and green grass. It was a building made of brick without windows and closed doors with locks that bolted shut behind him.

Tonight, he wasn't taking her to bed. He was taking somewhere where it would only be them.

Dante followed Emma inside.

The jolt of metal reverberated in the silence.

'You've locked the doors?'

'No one will enter now,' he answered. 'Only a select few know of its existence. But…'

'But?'

'Now, if they try to enter, they will know it's occupied.'

A long tunnel stretched out before her. Red fluorescent lights flickered above. Shadows blinked into focus in pink hues. She moved forward. Reached out and touched the wall. Let her fingers travel through the winding foliage climbing upwards. But climbing to where?

'What is this place?' she said, and she felt the tightness, the anticipation threading through her limbs.

'You'll see,' he said, his voice low and deep, echoing in the dark silence.

Heat rushed against her nape. He was so close, two feet behind her, maybe a little more, and yet he was so far away.

It was an imaginary whisper of his breath on her skin. But she felt it. The closeness of him. The heat driving her forward. The presence behind her pushing her to an unknown end.

'I'll see?' she asked.

'Yes,' he said. 'This is a place I come to when I want to be alone.'

'But you aren't alone.'

'I know.'

Her heart faltered. Her pulse beat without a steady throb, only an echo of it.

'And do you bring others here when you want to be alone?' she asked, her chest tightening. Painfully.

'Never.'

'Never?'

'Only now,' he said. 'Only *you*.'

Blood rushed through her veins. Her heart ham-

mered at the confirmation that she was the only one
to come here with him.

It meant something, didn't it? Even though she had
no idea where he'd brought her or where he was taking her. Or what she'd find when she came to the end.

'What do you do when you come here?'

'Eat.'

Still, his voice carried. A physical torture that did
not touch her skin. But it pierced into flesh. Drove
inside her.

'But there aren't any restaurants here,' she said
over her shoulder, walking forward.

'There are several hundred,' he corrected. *Jidō-
hanbaiki.*'

'Is that a restaurant? *Where?* I can't see it,' she
said, turning her gaze to the long walls at her sides.
'There are no people. No chefs. No waiters. There
are only—'

She paused.

There was a door.

And he closed in on her now. Stood behind her.
Inches away instead of feet.

'Go inside,' he urged.

She raised her hand to the silver looped handle.
Touched it. But she didn't pull, didn't push.

She lingered in this dark place where it was only
the two of them standing still in the darkness. Together.

He moved. Closer. Still not touching her. But the
distance between them, instead of centimetres, became millimetres and she couldn't breathe for the

need to turn and press herself into him. Into his chest. Into the breadth and bulk of him, and—

He shifted. Turned the distance, the space between them, into nothing, and touched her.

His fingertips feathered her cheek, pushed the hair behind her ear, and he leaned in farther, until his breath was real, hot beneath her earlobe.

'Don't you want to go inside?'

'What's in there?' she breathed.

'It will be only us.' His chest rose, and hers rose with it.

She pushed at the handle, and the door opened.

Warm yellow light infiltrated the darkness. She stepped forward and instantly regretted it as she moved away from the heat of him.

She longed to turn around. Return to him, to his arms. To surrender to this burn in her gut. To the flame growing brighter inside her. Fiercer by the second.

She stepped onto an over-polished white-and-black-speckled marble floor.

The quaintness of the homely potted plants, standing tall in every corner, the mismatched chairs, and well-worn tables, the pictures hung on the walls of smiling faces eating, a different delicacy in each photograph, the white bowls stacked high on a dark breakfast bar, consumed her.

She couldn't help it. She stepped farther into the room.

'You come here?' she asked. 'When you want to be alone?'

'Yes,' he confirmed, and she felt him enter the space with her. Fill the room with his presence.

She looked at the various coloured and sized rectangular machines standing in front of each wall but the photo wall.

Eyes wide, she turned to him. 'Vending machines?'

'Jidō-hanbaiki.' He nodded. *'Jihanki* for short.'

'Why here?'

'Why not here?' He hooked a brow. 'They are a cultural phenomenon here,' he explained. 'Vending machines can be found…everywhere. But inside these walls, you can be anywhere in the world with a press of a button. Anything you long to taste, to drink. From the most decadent ingredients to the most mundane. They are here. In this room.'

'But if you want something, you can have it in any room you like,' she said. 'Anywhere in the world you like.'

She ran her fingers through her hair, looked at him and then at the machines. So many of them. Several hundred choices of what to eat, what part of the world she wanted to taste, and yet she would be in one room. In one place.

'I thought you might enjoy this.'

'But why this room?' Her brow furrowed. 'Why this—' her eyes wandered, roamed the normality of it '—this place?'

'It is something different,' he said, and came to her. Lifted his hand, his fingers, and coiled a loose lock of hair around his finger. 'It is my garden.'

She frowned. 'Your garden?'

He swallowed thickly, and she watched the drag of his Adam's apple with bated breath.

'First, we will eat. Then I will tell you a story about a boy who found a place. A room. *A garden.*' The pressure on her scalp increased as his fingers tugged, not intentionally, not to hurt. But she felt the tension in his fingers. In his body. 'And I will explain why I have brought you here with me—why it had to be *here.*' He released the lock of hair. But her scalp still tingled. Her skin.

He turned his back on her. And breathlessly, she watched him.

Dante moved to the breakfast bar. The bowls clinked as he removed two from the stack. Removed cutlery from the stainless-steel containers holding them.

He moved again. One step after another, and he placed the bowls on the table. Set the cutlery aside each bowl and moved to a machine. Lifted his hand and pressed a button.

The machine whirled.

Emma didn't speak. Didn't move. She pretended to be invisible. A fly on the wall in a moment of Dante's life, his world, a place he had found where he could be alone. Wanted to be alone. And yet he'd invited her inside. It felt precious to be here. She felt precious. *Wanted.*

The aroma of ginger filled the air as the machine delivered a cup. He repeated the procedure until Dante retrieved two cups. He moved back to the bowls he'd prepared and poured the liquid inside each bowl.

'Chicken and ginger soup,' he said. He exhaled heavily. Pulled out the ordinary wooden chair, with a high back and no arms.

'Sit down, Emma.' She did, and he took his seat in front of her. Their eyes met. 'Eat.'

Together they picked up their spoons, dipped them into the soup and in sync, brought them to their lips.

It was a togetherness she'd never experienced, but her mother had craved it. Simple meals enjoyed by two. In companionable silence. In mutual understanding— the world outside could wait. Because the world outside was cold. Lonely.

The silence ricocheted in her ears. The comfortableness of it. The warmth. The realisation formed as clear as the broth before her. She could be anywhere in the world, anywhere she desired with a press of a button. And yet, she desired only to be with him. In this place. Safe in his company. Safe in their marriage. Safe with him.

Dante placed his spoon down on the worn table. 'My father employed an army to raise me. A high turnover of staff to feed me from the moment I was pulled from my mother's womb,' he told her. And she felt the pull of emotion in his words. The way he had to drag them from deep inside him. And she understood how hard that was. Understood because she had felt that way on the terrace of their hotel, when she had told him her story. Her story that she'd told no one else. But him. And so she didn't speak. She opened her ears and listened to his story.

'Nannies. Teachers. *Staff*,' he continued, his voice dark and heavy And it pushed itself through her consciousness. 'They were always around. Always talking. Always...*there*.' His face twisted into something ugly. 'And yet they were also not really there. At least not for me. They did not care for the boy in their charge, or for the teenager, the young man I became. Over the years, one face blended into several others. A name didn't matter because they all answered to one man. They answered to my father. To the rules he had set out for how to raise me.

'Whether I was in Italy, Switzerland or Nepal, they followed. Whether it was in a country estate in England, a castle in Sicily, a penthouse suite in Japan... I was surrounded by people. I was never alone. Never away from the noise—'

'So, you found your own garden?'

'I found a place,' he corrected. 'A room where I could choose to be. Not a place where my father ordered other people to take me. It was a different place in each city, each town. Whether it was a cafe in the village. A bookstore in a cobbled street. A room on a street no map knew. I entered it because I chose to be there. I paid them to close the door behind me. I—'

'You sneaked out in the dead of night to escape.'

Her heart pounded. They were the same. Him and her. And for him to confess that was big, she knew. They'd both been abandoned, in one form or another. Left to fend for themselves. But they had found each other. Created something…something that was theirs. Normal. *Unique*.

'You escaped,' she said and exhaled unsteadily, 'being alone in a house full of people who didn't care while your father conquered the world. Just for a while. Just for a time, you forgot the hardness. The loneliness. You created a world where all was quiet. Where all was still. A safe place where *you* wanted to be. You ruled over it, not your father, and you dictated who could enter. Who—'

'And I chose you,' he said. 'We chose this marriage. Because we wanted the same things. *Want* the same things. No borrowed beds. No temporary places to find respite. We share a house where we understand—'

'Each other?' she asked.

'I know you, and you know me,' he said and never had anyone known her.

He was on her side, wasn't he? They wanted the same things. *Needed* them. A safe place they could share together where love had no home, but she did. She had a home.

She wanted this. This marriage. She wanted to stay. Stay where she had someone. Had him on her side.

'I brought you here to show you, prove to you that I didn't need our marriage to be a safe haven, that I had places I could come for that. But I have realised that although our marriage has never required it, although we have never wanted it before, we can be each other's safe place.

'It was safer before to leave the noise and other people outside. Because if I let them inside, if I learned their faces, learned their names, then they could leave. And them leaving would be too much. It was safer to not get attached. To keep them at arm's length. I kept *you* at arm's length,' he admitted.

'You kept me at arm's length?'

He nodded. 'Yes, and I was wrong.'

'Wrong?'

'To shut you out,' he confessed. 'We are the same. Our needs are the same. We are no risk to each other. I can be your garden, Emma.'

He scowled. A thousand emotions flashed on his tightly drawn features. And she couldn't read a single one.

'I *am* your garden,' he corrected, 'and you are mine. Our marriage is the safe place. Our marriage is a safeguard against all we do not want. Love. Emotional attachment. We are each other's safe place, Emma.'

'A safe place?' She looked at him. His dark hair was neatly combed over to the side; soft and billowy from being newly washed, it teased at his ears. Dark stubble covered his cheeks, his sharply angled jaw. Leading her eyes down his throat to his shoulders, broad and sheathed by a suit jacket that sat on him like a second skin, over the fitted black T-shirt revealing the tautness of his bronze chest.

'Yes,' he said.

She lifted her gaze back to his.

She'd found what she thought she'd never wanted.

Safety with a man.

With him.

The organ inside her chest fluttered as wildly as a million bees buzzing towards home. Towards their queen. And it didn't matter to them. To the bees, where home was, because home was their queen.

Home was right in front of her, wasn't it?

He was her garden. *He* was her safe place. He was giving her everything she'd always wanted. And things she'd never considered as a way to get them. A relationship. Marriage.

But he was showing her he could provide for her needs. From her simplest need to her most extravagant. The whole world surrounded them. He was offering her the world. He was offering *his* world. A safe place. Where she would be warm. Cared for. Protected. Wanted. But not loved. Because neither of them wanted that.

'And maybe this is the reason you left. I kept you on the outside. But I know your face. I know your name. You can come inside, Emma. You can stay. Because in here, and in our house, in our bed, I will give you what you need. Security. A safe place from the hardness. I wanted you to know, for you to understand, when I take you to bed, when I possess your body, I can give you what it is you need. To know that I can provide it by giving you everything you don't have.'

Suddenly, Emma was slammed with the last five years of her life.

Her spoon clanked into the empty bowl.

Emma remembered everything. The breakdown of her marriage. Her reasons for staying. Her reasons for leaving.

She knew why she'd left. *She remembered.*

She stood. The chair screeched backwards. She'd left, abandoned their marriage, the contract they'd agreed to, because she *had* started to get emotionally invested in their marriage. She had wanted more than either of them had agreed to give one another. She had wanted this man she'd sworn never to need. Never to—

'What is it?' Dark and intense, his eyes probed hers. 'What's wrong?'

Emma closed her eyes. She needed a minute, a moment, to collect herself. Because she was hurting.

Her chest, her heart, ached.

She heard the slide of his chair. His footfall coming towards her. Firm fingers claimed her chin. She opened her eyes. Met his. Dark and probing.

'What is it?' he demanded roughly.

'I don't feel well.' Her core trembled in deep, rhythmic spasms. 'I'd like to go back to the hotel. I'd like to…'

She didn't know.

She'd got emotionally attached.

She'd broken the rules.

But he didn't know that.

To him, she'd just left. She'd abandoned him. Like his mother. His father. She'd left him alone, without a safe place, without explanation.

And still he'd come for her.

Still, he was here.

And he was wrong; she *was* a risk. It wasn't safe for him in this place with her. She wanted all the things he'd locked outside. And she'd brought them inside with her.

'I'm sorry,' she breathed, because she was. Sorry for breaking the rules. Sorry for needing him. For wanting him in ways they'd never agreed to. Sorry for wanting what he didn't want. Sorry for letting him lock the doors behind her, for letting him learn her name, her face, when she was the danger. She was everything he didn't want. And he'd let her in. He'd—

Dante released her chin. 'You are exhausted, Emma.' He shook his head. 'I should have let you sleep.'

He picked her up and held her against him. And she let him carry her back the way they'd come. She closed her eyes. Pushed her face into the crook of his neck.

She wouldn't let the tears fall.

She wouldn't cry.

But she knew when they left this place, there was no going back now for either of them.

CHAPTER ELEVEN

DANTE CLIPPED EMMA'S seat belt and told the driver to take them back to the Cappetta Continental.

She collapsed against the seat and watched out of the window. Everything looked different. Felt different. The sleeping streets were too grey, too dim. The city lights, the busy billboards of flashing images, nonsensical.

Emma hadn't only betrayed herself. She'd betrayed Dante. And now she understood just how deeply.

She'd run away, abandoned him, without explanation. She'd left him alone in a house with nothing but empty noise. With faces of people who didn't care, who would walk out of his life without a backward glance. Staff who were there to meet his every need, but who didn't know his face. They didn't know his name. They did not know him.

Emma knew him.

Her stomach hurt. She wanted to sob at the emptiness she hadn't recognised before. This emptiness that had only ever been absent when he'd been with her. Inside her. Filled the hollow where he'd branded her. Ruined her.

And she was ruined, wasn't she?

She'd ruined everything because she'd caught feelings. So why then did she not feel ruined? Why was she warm? Why was she—

She was a fool.

The car stopped outside the hotel, ablaze in pink light. Dante stepped out of his side and opened her door. She looked up, met the questioning dark brown of his eyes, and she understood her time was up. She had to tell him her memory had returned. She knew why she'd left.

'Shall I carry you?'

She shook her head. How could she let him carry her, hold her, when she was the enemy? When she was everything he didn't want? He never should have taken her to his place. He never should have let her in.

'No.' She swallowed it down. The lump in her throat felt as though it was blocking her airway, making it difficult to breathe. She had no choice. She was going to have to reveal herself. Expose her crimes. And then it would be over.

They would be over.

'Come.' He offered her his hand. Long, thick bronze fingers reaching for her. How many times had he claimed her hand? Held it? Comforted her when she did not deserve it? She did not deserve him. His softness. His trust. She was not his safe place. She was not his garden. And he could no longer be hers.

Emma reached out her hand to him, and he

claimed it. Supported her as she stepped out of the car, and together they walked into the hotel, to the lift. And she saw none of the hotel lobby. Only him. Only his hand. The strength of it closing around hers and keeping her steady.

But she was not steady. Inside, she trembled. Inside, she knew, after tonight, after she told him the truth, he'd never hold her hand again.

The steel doors closed, sealing them inside.

Her throat ached. She swallowed repeatedly, trying to soothe it. To prepare it for the story she knew she must tell. But she wasn't prepared. She wasn't ready.

How different her body felt from the last time they'd been in here together just a few hours earlier. It wasn't anticipation flooding through her in waves as it had been before. It was a heaviness. A breathless dread. She was rigid, sweating beneath her coat.

Higher and higher the lift climbed until the ping of arrival boomed into the air between them.

Hand in hand, side by side, they moved through the open doors—

'Dante,' she said, and he stopped. Turned. And it was acute. The realisation. The piercing pain in her chest. These would be their last moments together.

'Kiss me,' she said, because she needed just one kiss. One last kiss. To feel the rush of his lips. The softness of his mouth. And then she would tell him. Then she would let him go.

She'd let him close the door on them. Lock her out. Because what else could she do? He'd never lied to her. He'd never broken the rules. But she had. She was breaking them by being here. By not being strong enough, the day she'd left Mayfair, to tell him the truth, and ask for a divorce.

'You must sleep, Emmy.' Dark eyes held hers. 'And when you are rested—' he stepped into her space and the heat of him, the scent of him, a smell unique to him, entered her pores and her heart sang '—we will talk about what's next. What's next for us.'

He lifted his hand, and with an open palm, he placed it on her cheek. Cradled it. Swiped the pad of his thumb across her cheekbone. And she wanted to lean into his softness. Lean against his strength because she was weak.

She was her mother.

Dante would never—

Is it love?

Was that what she was feeling now? Because she might not have felt it when she left. But it felt different now. Stronger.

Not the lie of love she'd watched her mother chase all her life, but the love in her mum's books. The books Emma had stolen to read in the garden. Stories of a love that recognised not just the flesh, but the person underneath it. Saw beneath skin and bone and stared at their soul. A mirror image of themselves.

Was this what her mother had longed for all those years? What she'd craved? Waited for to her detriment? For someone to let her in. To know what each other needed and to respond to that need with care and consideration. To keep each other safe from the noise—from the hardness—and take care of each other softly.

Dante had treated her softly. Gently, he'd claimed her and their marriage when she didn't even remember what she'd done. She'd run fast and far away from him. From all the things growing inside her. And still they grew. Her heart bulged in its confines. Strained to be released from its bony cage.

'Kiss me, please,' she begged. *'Now.'* She needed his mouth on hers. She needed to say with her lips what she couldn't find the words to say. Didn't want to say.

'One kiss,' he breathed, and it was all she wanted. One last kiss before he thrust her from him. Called her a liar, a betrayer. An infiltrator. And—

His hand slid down her arm, sneaked beneath her coat and claimed her hip. He pulled, and she followed. Let him mould her body to his.

How perfectly they fit. How perfectly her body aligned with his.

She lifted her hand to his shoulder, clung to it— *to him*—and watched his mouth descend. Felt the warmth of his breath feather her lips. And she opened for him. Parted her lips for his.

She closed her eyes as his hands claimed her face. She pressed her palms to his cheeks and held his face just as carefully. Just as softly.

His lips met hers. Brushed against them so softly. So tenderly. And she wanted to sob—wail her distress, but she held it in, pushed her mouth against his harder and thrust her tongue inside his mouth. And she felt it. The rush. The headiness of his possession as his tongue pushed inside her mouth and met hers. And she kissed him. Harder. Deeper. She pushed all those feelings inside her chest into this kiss.

She let him taste the ferociousness of them. Of these feelings she'd run away from in Mayfair. She'd fought it that day. This knowing she wanted more. Needed more of him. Until she could no longer fight it and ran away before she could confess it.

Emma didn't fight it now. She let it drive her. Her tongue. Her kiss. She kissed him with need, with longing for all the things she wanted and knew he didn't. She kissed him with her goodbye. She kissed him with everything she'd never allowed herself to feel. With warmth. With passion. With need. *With love.*

Something fundamental had shifted between them. Changed. They were different. *She* was different. *She* was changed. And he'd done it to her. He'd shown her tenderness, passion, cared for her softly, and she'd transformed because of him.

He was right. The night they'd met the sex had been carnal. Their relationship passionate. Intense. *More.* And that's all they'd ever wanted, all they'd ever claimed from one another.

But tonight, and since her fall, he'd been...*different*. Softer and more patient. Gentle. Never had their relationship been gentle. Never had they talked. Never had she asked questions. Never had he allowed it. Never had he been around long enough. Never had she understood why everything they'd agreed to meant so very much to them both. Why, they were a match in and out of bed.

She understood now.

'Emmy…' he moaned into her mouth, and she ached. Her heart ached. He knew her. He knew her name.

She tore her mouth away from his, and it was agony to end their last kiss.

'Dante,' she began and kissed the tip of his chin. 'Dante,' she repeated and kissed his cheek. 'Dante,' she said again, and applied her lips to the softness of his other cheek. 'I know your name, Dante,' she said, and this time the tears built as she brushed her lips across his closed eyelid and then the other. 'I know your face,' she said, and dropped her hand from his face. From the warmth of him. She stepped back, dislodging his hands, his body, from hers. 'I know who you are,' she said, moving backwards, back towards the lift. And it hurt to be so far away from him, and yet so close. 'I know *you*,' she said, and it trembled, her voice. Her words.

They recognised each other, didn't they? Were drawn to each other without rhyme or reason. Without logic. Their bodies knew, if not their minds, not their hearts, that they belonged together. And they'd lied to themselves, created rules and signed contracts to make the illogical logical. They'd given themselves a way to understand it. This connection that ran more than skin-deep. It was more than the sharing of heat between flesh. Bodies. It was deeper. It was a connection of the souls.

Soulmates.

She recognised his soul, didn't she? She'd recognised it the very first night, and she'd thrown caution to the wind, broken her every vow to be with him. To have more of him.

Fate had slammed them together when the probability of them ever meeting was not only improbable, but it should have been impossible.

And yet it had happened.

They had met.

They had recognised each other.

He knew her.

He'd always known her.

But this she must do.

Confess.

'Come to bed, Emmy.'

It would be so easy to pretend. To walk inside their suite and follow him to bed. To climb inside the sheets and wrap her body around his. It would be so easy to shut her eyes and claim one more night. To keep him in the dark. To shield him from the truth that would end them.

'I can't,' she croaked, denying him, denying herself, because if she did, if she stayed, if she went to bed with him, she knew what the jail sentence would be.

She'd lived it. Understood exactly what she'd be signing up for. And she'd only fall deeper for him. Get deeper into a situation that would echo her mum's. And she knew how that ended.

So she couldn't follow him. She couldn't pretend even for one more night. Because if she did, it would be worse than loving him. It would be knowing she loved him. It would be hope that one day he'd love her back. And hope killed.

If she followed him, if she waited for his love, it would kill her.

She wasn't naive anymore. She'd left him because she'd been afraid of her developing emotional attachment to him. *But now...* She understood him better than she ever had in their marriage. Understood herself more. And what she'd tried to stomp out and forget the day she'd left Mayfair had grown beyond attachment.

She was his worst nightmare come true.

She was emotionally attached.

She was his soulmate.

She was in love with him.

And she'd been fighting it for months. She'd still been fighting it when he'd come for her in the hospital. She'd clung to her younger self. That naive young woman who was certain she wanted nothing like that for herself. She'd had rules in place. Knew what love did to a person.

And even without her memory, she'd needed a way out too. In case she'd needed it again.

She'd demanded a divorce if she wanted one, as he'd demanded a get-out clause in their marriage contract. He'd needed it as much as she had. Be-

cause his wounds ran as deep as hers, didn't they?
And she didn't know how to mend him. Mend herself. Mend them.

She knew what he wanted. He'd never lied to her.
Never failed to deliver what he'd promised. But the
goal posts had changed. She was changing them. She
wanted something different.

She wanted a real marriage.

'Why not?' he asked, his eyes pinning her and
penetrating hers deeply. 'Why can't you come to bed
with me?'

Her time was up.

The end was coming and she would summon it
with her confession.

Unless this wasn't the end of them.

It was a beginning.

She should have used her words three months ago.
But she had been afraid. Afraid his needs would not
align with hers.

And she was still afraid now.

But he was her match.

And she was his.

Together, what if they could beat the fear?

Together, what if they could learn to love and define it for themselves?

Together, what if they could transcend?

Hope bloomed inside her.

'I need to tell you something.'

'Should I call a doctor?' he asked, and she saw it.
The flash of worry.

He cared.

She shook her head.

It wasn't enough.

'I remember.'

His mouth opened, those competent lips she wanted to kiss again and again, until she was breathless with his kiss. *Now.* In this penthouse suite in Japan. She wanted to kiss his cheeks again, his stubbled jaw, his eyelids; she wanted to tell him she knew him again. She knew his face. And she wanted to take him somewhere too. Somewhere new, where they both could live in safety, wrapped in the warmth of love. To prove to him that they were the same. They belonged together.

She closed her eyes, because it was easier to confess when she wasn't looking at him. At the face of the man she loved.

'I remember everything,' she confessed, and her heart raged in a deafening roar. 'I remember why I left. Why I ran away from you—' And she faltered, shame stabbing into her core. Because she had been weak, and she had abandoned him like everyone else in his life. She would not abandon him now, not without explanation at least.

'I'm sorry. I'm sorry I left you alone. I'm sorry I—' Slowly, she opened her eyes. Looked at him.

She would not hide anymore. She would own her feelings and she would survive them.

He deserved her love.

She deserved his.

They deserved each other's.

And so she let him in. His dark gaze, Emma let it in behind the walls she'd built.

'I was afraid,' she confessed.

'Of what?' he asked, and she heard the hardness in his voice. The resistance to whatever was happening between them. Because it was happening. The air was thick with it. With change. With possibilities.

'I was scared of you, Dante,' she confessed. 'Of what you made me feel. I feared for myself.'

'I've never given you reason to fear—'

'And yet I was afraid,' she said. 'I broke the rules. I got emotionally attached. I caught feelings. I am having feelings right now. Big feelings. Scary feelings, Dante. And I am afraid still. Afraid when I tell you, when I confess what it is I have done—what I am doing, what I feel—you will send me away.'

'Come to bed, Emma,' he said, and this time, it was not a request. It was a demand. And he moved towards her. And all she could see was him. Dante Cappetta. Her husband. The man who had given her the tools to heal herself. The man who held her hand. Her body. The man who took care of her.

And she wanted to take care of him. She wanted to hold his hand. She wanted to shelter him from the hardness with her body. But she wanted his heart. She wanted to put it in a safe place and hold it with her own. She wanted to love him and she wanted him to love her.

'In bed, I will claim your big feelings with my lips,' he said, and took another step closer. 'I will drive myself inside you until the bigness of your feelings can escape. As we have always done. When we make love. When I love your body, there is no fear. No escape from the flame within us. In bed, we let it roar, let it consume us.' Another step. 'Do not be afraid of it. Do not fear—'

'*Stop!*' she cried, and halted him with a raised open palm. 'Our contract is void, Dante. I broke—'

'It does not matter. I do not want to know. You are here now, Emma. We can continue as we agreed.'

'We can't,' she corrected.

'We can,' he rasped. 'Here with me, you can have it all. Physical pleasure. Security. Safety in my arms. Everything I have promised is yours.'

'It isn't enough anymore,' she admitted, her chest tight and heaving. 'I lo—'

'Emma, don't,' he warned, his every feature tight. Drawn. *Pained*.

But she would. All her life she'd been running from her feelings, her needs, her secret desires. Afraid she'd turn out like her mum. Unloved and unwanted. But Emma was wanted. And she wanted to be loved.

Loved by him.

'I'm in love with you,' she said, and it felt freeing. Liberating. So she said it again, 'I love—'

'Do not say it again, Emma,' he warned darkly.

'I know right now you're afraid.'

'I am not afraid.' His black gaze intense beneath arched brows, he said, 'You have betrayed me, Emma. You have betrayed us both.'

'I believed that too. It's why I left. Why I wrote

that note. I knew I'd betrayed us both. But those two versions of us, *they* betrayed *us*,' she corrected,

'There is no *us*,' he said.

'Our parents. Our pasts. The ghosts of both, they are dragging us down, forcing us to deny our feelings, making us hide them underneath our fear. They are defining our lives, our relationships, because of their mistakes.'

'Nobody defines me. I live my life my way, by my rules.'

'You know that isn't true,' she said. 'Your mother was the reason you had a vasectomy when you were all but a child.'

'I was a man.'

'You were a boy entering manhood the only way he could,' she rejected. 'You severed any potential threat that a child could be used against you. Because you have been taught, as I have, that people use other people for their own selfish desires. You've learned not to trust. Not to let anyone get close. Not to love anyone, or let them love you, because ultimately, they will betray you. That's why you have so many rules. It's why we had a contract. So you wouldn't get attached. Because all the people who should have been attached to you emotionally, unconditionally, they abandoned you. So you created a world full of safety nets and get-out clauses for when things got too real. Too risky—'

'Do not twist my words, Emma,' he said. His voice was a low hiss of warning. 'I meant, *I mean*, exactly what I said.'

'I know,' she soothed.

'Do not try to placate me.'

'I'm not. I meant every word I have ever said to you too, and we were both wrong,' she said. 'I won't hide under false promises anymore. Or fake rules. To live a safe existence. To simply survive this life I'm meant to be living because I'm afraid. I will be free of them. I will exorcise those that wish to trap me in a life of fear. Of rules. Of contracts. Those who would deny me what I deserve. And I deserve to be cared for when I'm hurt. To be treated softly when I need soft. To be kissed passionately whenever I want. I will have it all. I will be loved.'

'Do not use words when you do not understand the definition. We both know that love is a lie. There is only lust. There is only the body—'

'I don't believe that anymore. What about the soul?' she asked. 'You recognised mine the night we met. I recognised yours. We recognised each other. We were drawn to each other without rhyme or reason. Without logic. Our bodies knew, if not our minds, our hearts, that we belong together. We have lied to ourselves. We created rules and signed contracts to make the illogical logical. We gave ourselves a way to understand it. This connection between us. But it is deeper than sharing our bodies. We are—'

'Compatible,' he interjected. 'In bed.'

'We are soulmates.'

'You are deluded.'

'I am enlightened.'

'I will call the doctor.'

'And what will you tell him?' she asked. 'Your wife is in love with you?'

'You are not my wife,' he spat. 'You are an imposter.'

'You're right. I am. I'm not the woman you married. I'm not the woman content to be in a relationship where nothing but the physical means anything. But you are an imposter too. You have changed. You let me in, Dante. You took me to your place. You have done so many things our contract doesn't allow for. You came for me when I fell. You brought me to Japan. You trusted me, only me, enough to take me there tonight and tell me your story. I know how hard that was for you, because it was hard for me to tell you everything about myself the other night on the terrace. You love me, Dante,' she said, and prayed. Prayed everything she'd said was enough. Because she wanted to stay. With him. 'Even if you won't admit it to me, can't admit it to yourself.'

The pressure built behind her eyes, and she couldn't hold the tears back. They splashed onto her cheeks in hot, salty streams. There was too much to hold in. She did not want to say it. She did not want to leave. But she understood. She knew him. What this would cost him. But she was not her father. She would not use a language of lies to take what she needed from him if it meant he would lose himself. But—

'Is it such a great sacrifice, Dante?' she asked, and stifled the tears—wiped them away. She tilted her neck, straightened her spine—her shoulders. 'To let me love you? To love me in return?'

'I do not love you, Emma,' he said.

She wanted to block her ears. Close her eyes. 'Dante—'

'I have listened to you, and now you will listen to me,' he said. 'The contract was clear. I have been clear. And now it is over, Emma. I am ending it.' The coldness of his words, his voice, stabbed into her chest. Into her heart. And it cracked. Not a split. Not a fracture.

It was fatal.

A killing wound.

'I'm sorry,' she husked, because she was. She was sorry she couldn't lie. Couldn't pretend. She was sorry her feelings were too big for them both. 'I'll leave. Now.' And she dragged her eyes away from him, turned her body away from the only man she'd ever trusted. The only man she'd ever loved and wanted to love her back.

And it was agony.

It was like a death.

She took a step forward, and she felt it. Her heart breaking. But she would stem the flow. She would survive him. The way her mother hadn't survived her father. Because she at least was honest enough with herself to know what she needed. What she deserved. She was honest enough to walk away with the knowledge that he couldn't return her love.

Firm fingers caught her wrist. She looked up in to his eyes. And they blazed. His nostrils flared.

'You do not get to leave me ever again.'

* * *

Dante's chest heaved. His every muscle stretched tight.

He'd let her get too close. Let her become essential to his survival, let her become his air. But he would learn to breathe without her. This was the ultimate betrayal. He'd trusted her. Told her things. Shown her things. He'd allowed her to get too close. She'd taken his power. Dulled his defences with her tears and tales.

'Do you know why I came to get you from the hospital?' He stepped closer to her to prove he could be near her without reaching out and touching her.

He would claim his power back.

'Because you care, Dante,' she said breathlessly. 'Because you love—'

'I came to *out* you.'

'Out me?'

'Expose you,' he said, and watched her pale face drain of colour.

'Expose me?' she gasped.

'It was not hard to work out, Emma, because you are all the same.'

'The same?'

'You all want more. You are no different from any of them.'

He'd been right all along.

She was playing with him.

She was a liar. She knew, as he did, that love didn't exist. And yet she used this word like ammunition. But her words would not pierce his armour. He would

not let her in. He would not let her leave. Abandon
him. *Again.*

'My mother. She was like you,' he said, and he
saw her frown, watched her lips compress, as she
waited for him to explain. So he continued, because
she needed to understand that he saw straight through
her.

'She married my father with a contract such as
ours. A marriage contract that stipulated the condi-
tions of their marriage. The rules. And my mother
used them to her advantage. She manipulated my
father into giving her a bigger settlement. She used
what she thought he wanted most and manipulated
him. I have never hidden how much I want you. I
never tried to hide the power you have over me. Even
without your memory, you have seen it. My desire to
keep you. And you use that admission against me.
But I will not be manipulated.'

'What is it you think I want from you if not what
I've asked for?' she said. 'I want your love. And I'm
willing to walk away without it.'

'And it is too big a payment,' he rasped. 'An impossible request. It does not exist. It is a lie.'

'But it does exist. You collected me from the hospital because of love. You have taken care of me with
love. You—'

'Kept my promise to you!' A roar built inside him.
And he wanted to release it. Call her names. Call her
a liar. A manipulator. 'And you have broken them all.
I told you my story of a boy—'

'A lonely boy.'

'And you have twisted everything I told you, and now you threaten to take away the one thing I want. *You*. So, what is it, Emma? Tell me,' he roared. 'What do you think I will give to you if you offer me love?'

'Love in return.'

'You are a liar.'

'Can't you see?' she asked, and there were her tears again. And she placed her open palm on his chest. Over his heart. A reflection of where their relationship had started.

And the organ that gave him life, it was betraying him. It pumped too hard. Too fast under the pressure of her fingers. 'They, our parents, are dragging something beautiful into their ugly mistakes. I have never played with you or toyed with you. I have been honest with you since the night we met. I *am* being honest with you now. And I know what I'm saying is against the rules. But I have changed. *We* have changed. Let me in, Dante. Let me inside. Let me love you.'

'No.' He shrugged off her hand. Her hold on him. He would have his power back and he would have it now.

'I came into this marriage with nothing, and I'll leave with what I came with, because I don't need any of it. The things in Mayfair that I left behind in the first place, I don't want them,' she husked. 'I only want you. I only need *you*. This isn't a plan of deception. I am not trying to deceive you. I am not your mother. I… I love you. And I know you love me. But I won't…'

'You are wrong, Emma. I do not love you. I do not

want your love. I will not beg you to stay. I will not
accept your lies. Your broken promises in place of
something we both know doesn't exist. And yet you
use it, this word *love* as though it means something
to me. It means *nothing*.'

His fingers were still clenched around her small
wrist. He looked down to where he held her, tethered
her to him, and his fingers ached with every demand
he made for them to loosen. To release her.

'And now *you* mean nothing to me.'

He let her wrist go, and he couldn't inhale.

He could not feed his lungs enough air.

He could not breathe deeply enough.

'But I keep my promises, Emma,' he said, because
who was he without rules, without the playbook? He
was weak. He would not be weak. But it flashed in
his head. Emma's hardness. Birmingham. The hospital. The blood—

'Tomorrow, I will call a car to collect you. Book
the jet to take you back to England. The Mayfair
house is yours. The deeds will be at the house when
you arrive.'

'Dante—'

'You will be financially secure for the rest of your
life.'

'I—'

'I do not want to listen to you anymore, Emma. I
do not want to be anywhere near anything you have
touched. Tainted with your lies and broken promises.
Everything in the house is yours. I do not want any

of it. I do not want—' he looked at his hand, at the gold band that signified their union '—this.'

He took it off, his wedding ring, and displayed it in the air between them and held her gaze, ignored the tears streaming down her cheeks and the instinct to use his thumb to wipe them away.

He dropped the ring to the floor.

She gasped.

'I am leaving *you*,' he said, and the words were fire in his mouth. 'And there will be no second chances, Emma. I will not come for you. I will not wait for you to come to me with some tale of woe. It is over. We are—'

'Dante, *please*.'

He shut his ears. Blocked the Emma-shaped hole in his head. He would not let her. He did not need her. He did not want her.

Liar.

He walked past her. And it hurt. The pull of her against him. The urge to give in to temptation. To go to her and not to step around her, to enter the lift and keep on going. To walk away from her.

'Where are you going?'

His hand on the button, his feet stalled. He did not turn. He would not look.

He'd go where he should have the night they'd met. He never should have clasped her hand. Claimed her lips. Possessed her body. Because that night she'd possessed him, his body, his mind, until everything he did was unnatural to him.

'As far away from you as I can,' he said, and

firmly pressed the button, walked inside the opening doors and kept his back turned on the lie of Emma. The lie of their marriage. The lie she had turned it into with her broken promises.

Because if he looked, if he watched the doors close on her, doubt would blur the edges of his conviction. Doubt would weaken him. But he was resolved.

He did not want her love.

He was not changed.

He was not weak.

The doors closed.

A coldness tore through his flesh and entered his bones. His lungs.

He placed a hand on the mirrored wall. He held himself on his feet.

There was no oxygen.

He was cold.

He was alone.

And Dante couldn't breathe.

CHAPTER TWELVE

DANTE HADN'T SLEPT.

For six weeks, he'd searched for it. The rush. Adrenaline. *The high.*

He'd searched for the man he was. Jumped out of planes. Climbed mountains. He'd sought the monks in the hills. He'd meditated. He'd prayed. To all the gods. Old and new. None had answered. Still, he could not find it. He was lost to himself. Displaced. Alone on a ledge. Cold. And he didn't want to be cold. He wanted to be warm. But *nothing* warmed him.

Dante scrubbed his hands over his face. His beard was full, and his hair was too long. He closed his eyes. Raked his fingers through his hair and pulled at the roots.

Why wouldn't it just die?

Dante opened his eyes and stared at the papers in front of him. At the empty signature boxes.

The divorce papers were ready.

By every rule in the playbook, they should already be divorced. Japan never should have happened. But he'd allowed it to happen. Instigated it, even. Bent every rule to seduce her. To make her want to stay.

And she'd wanted to stay.

He was the one who had sent her away this time.

He'd projected every single childhood trauma onto her shoulders when the weight was not hers to bear. It was *his*.

Because he did have trauma, didn't he? She'd pulled it from the places he'd hidden it. Exposed it. The cruelties that raised boys and broke men.

And he was broken. A shell of the man he knew he once was. Because he had hurt her on purpose. And he could not forgive himself for that. Even though it was the right thing to do. He'd broken his promise to keep her safe. To protect her. He could not protect her from him. From his fear of attachment. Of belonging to another and watching them leave.

And so he had left first.

Left *her* behind.

Abandoned her.

But he did not feel powerful.

He was not himself. The rules, the playbook, were obsolete, because none of it was working for him.

Had they ever worked? How had they served him? He'd lived an exhilarating life. But it had been a lonely life.

Until her.

And she'd let him into her garden. He'd seduced her, lulled her into the falsity that she was safe with him inside. He'd assured her it was safe. He would not crush the blooms. He would not crush her.

But he was a snake, and he had bitten her. A venomous bite. And no, their marriage was dead. Because he couldn't accept that she had changed him. That he was—

In love?

She hadn't contested the agreed settlement. She had not sought more than he'd already promised. She had not even demanded a divorce.

She was not his mother.

She'd only wanted to *love* him.

To be loved in return.

He was a fool. A *changed* fool. Because what did he know of love? Only what she'd told him. Shown him. That she was his soulmate.

How could he let her in with these feelings? Big and scary, they haunted him. Her confession. Her love.

His stomach clenched.

All that was required was two signatures. And then it would be over. She would be gone. Forever.

He should not be hesitating. He should not be letting doubt in where it did not belong. She did not belong to him. He could not keep her safe. He could not meet her needs. He did not know this love. He did not know himself.

After today, after he signed the papers, he'd be able to breathe. They would finally be at an end. Divorced. He'd watch her sign the papers too, and only then would he be free of her. Only then would what it was that they shared die. And he would find himself again.

You'll be alone.

As he always had been.

The plane landed without ceremony. Dante collected the papers and carried them in his too-tight grip. He descended the stairs and got into the waiting car.

Ten minutes and she would sign.

Emma was still afraid.

The first time she'd left Dante, she'd gone back to what she knew. Her life before him. Back to the estate, back to surviving, to start again. She'd worked any and every job the agency had offered her. She'd worked endlessly until exhaustion claimed all her senses. And she didn't have to think or *feel*. She didn't have to remember what she'd left behind. Or what was coming. Any second now.

The end.

Divorce.

In the back of her mind, in the fog of exhaustion, she'd known it would arrive.

Dante had said he hadn't wanted to stay in this house without her, and she understood it now, even more than she had on the plane.

It was agony. To be here. To see what she hadn't been able to see the night he'd brought her back from the hospital. The memories.

Dante lingered in every room. His scent followed her, infiltrated her every waking thought, and in sleep, he was there. In her dreams.

For six weeks, she'd wanted to lie on the floor and cry. Break things. And cry again.

She'd ruined everything because she'd uttered the one word she shouldn't have. Confessed to having that one feeling. A feeling she knew was too big for him. Too big for her too, because it consumed her. Even in Dante's absence, there was no escape from it. The yearning for it, for him. For what she'd had with him in Japan. Passion. Closeness. Intimacy.

She knew it was love now, even more so than she had known it the night she'd confessed it to him. And she would confess it again.

But Dante had never lied to her. Never manipulated her like her father had manipulated her mother. Dante had always told the truth. However blunt. However much she didn't want to hear it. He didn't lie. He did not break his promises.

He was never coming back.

But still she waited, still she stayed in this house, still she lived with the ghost of the man she loved, because she couldn't bear not to. Because a part of her still hoped even when she knew she shouldn't.

It terrified her, the depth of her feelings for him. And every day her love grew. It would not diminish. Every day it grew in certainty. In confidence. In strength. And that only made it worse. The pain. The knowing she had rushed him. She hadn't treated him as softly as he had treated her. She hadn't eased him in. She'd thrown her love at him and he hadn't known what to do with it, how to embrace this feeling he couldn't see. Didn't trust.

And now he didn't trust her.

But she trusted *him*. Trusted this love, however new, however fragile, to bring him back to her.

So still she was here. Still she waited. But the divorce papers hadn't arrived.

So she hoped he would find his way back to this place that was theirs. That was safe. She would not abandon it again. She would not leave it empty for him to find. She would not leave him to be alone.

So still she waited.

Still she loved.

There was a knock on the door.

She'd sent all the staff home; there was no one to answer it but her. So, barefoot, she ran down the stairs. Padded across the marble reception and silk rugs. To the door. She tugged it open—

Her mouth fell open. Never had she seen his hair so long, his beard so full. Never had he come to her in a T-shirt creased from travel. Jeans loose at the hips from too much wear. She searched his face. Noted the bruises under his bloodshot eyes.

The bud of hope inside her bloomed. She wanted to reach for him. Tell him it would be okay. He was safe here with her. But she was afraid. Afraid he wasn't here to stay.

And then she eyed the papers scrunched tightly in his hand. The bulge of his naked forearm...

He'd come to claim his divorce.

Not their marriage.

Not her.

And she felt it.

The death of hope.

CHAPTER THIRTEEN

DANTE STAGGERED. It hit him in waves. A breathless rush of emotion. Adrenaline. Warmth.

It hit him square in his chest and suddenly he could breathe again after what felt like an eternity.

And he gulped in the air that was finally hitting his lungs.

For weeks he'd searched. He'd jumped out of planes in order to feel something, anything. He'd prayed for it. For air. She had it. She had his air.

His chest squeezed.

And it was guttural. The noise rising in his chest. The rumble of pain. It scraped against his throat, clawed at the insides of his mouth and burst through his lips.

He groaned.

She stepped forward on her bare feet and reached for him.

'Dante.' She said his name in anguish. In distress. As though she had been waiting for him to arrive on her doorstep.

He stepped back.

She dropped her hand. And he felt the thump of it on her thigh. The withdrawal of her offer of kindness.

He didn't deserve it. Her touch. Her softness. Her concern.

'Come inside, Dante.'

He couldn't. He shook his head. Clenched his teeth. It hurt. It hurt to breathe. It hurt to be in front of her and not inhale her. Press his nose into her skin and let her scent feed him. Revive him.

But he couldn't reach out and touch the loose strands of hair falling from the knot on top of her head, couldn't tuck them behind her ear. He couldn't touch the pale flesh exposed beneath her burgundy camisole. The elegant column of her throat. Her naked shoulder. He could not trace his fingers down the beige lace sloping down her breasts. He could not get down on his knees and kiss her bare toes peeping out from beneath wide hemmed burgundy trousers.

Here he stood on the white stone steps, before the black door of the house he'd bought for her. To share with her. And he couldn't go inside.

It wasn't his house anymore.

He didn't belong here.

He'd abandoned it all.

Abandoned her.

Backwards, he descended the steps. Until he stood at the bottom of the five stone steps looking up at the life he could have had. The woman he wanted. Still. Now.

Every adventure, every job, he'd come back to

her. Back to this house. For her. She was his safe place. She was…

He searched her blue eyes, wide and watching him.

She was home.

She was warmth.

She was—

Waiting.

Regret clawed at his insides.

They could have made this house their place. A shared place of safety. Together.

A home.

Because home was *her*, he realised.

And he'd thrown it all away, something beautiful, a gift.

'I won't come inside,' he told her, even though he wanted to. He wanted in. 'This is your place now. Your safe place from the hardness, Emma. From the worry of surviving. And I will not enter it.' Tighter, his chest squeezed. The muscle that gave him life pounded without mercy. 'Unless you want me to.'

'Is that what you want?' she asked. 'To come inside?'

'I have no right to come in. I have no right to ask anything of you after Japan, after I—' pain seared through his gut '—left you.'

'You were scared.'

'And so were you, but you still found the strength to tell me a truth you knew I didn't want to hear. And I abandoned you. I left you alone with those big, scary feelings. I left you alone with all that *love*.'

He placed his open palm on his chest and kneaded it, because something was happening in his chest. Something—

'Your love felt like a heavy thing, Emma, and I'm sorry I did not hold it gently. It's such a precious thing. My hands didn't know how to hold such a thing delicately. So I dropped it. I hurt you. I didn't know another way. I didn't—'

They were all excuses.

He raised his eyes to the grey morning sky, but he wouldn't pray. No one could help him. Not the rules. Not the playbook. They were meaningless. Because never had they warned him about Emma. Never had they warned him about love.

And he loved her.

He needed her.

She was his air.

He would end this agony.

'I was wrong,' he hissed. 'Wrong to compare you to my mother. You are *nothing* like her. You are not *them*, my parents. But they live inside me, Emma. *They* are my demons. I let them dictate my reactions, my responses, to you. You were right about so many things. The rules. The risks. I never should have put my demons on your shoulders. Your beautiful shoulders that have already carried so much. Too much. I too want to exorcise them. Exorcise all those who would make me live this life in fear. But I am afraid, Emma.'

He fell to his knees before her then. On the pavement. And he looked up the stone steps at the life he wanted.

The wife he would keep.

If she would let him.

If she would let him in.

'What are you afraid of, Dante?' she asked. Still she stood in the doorway, unmoved, keeping him out.

'I'm afraid of you, Emma,' he admitted. 'I am afraid of myself. And I'm afraid when I tell you. When I confess what it is I have done. What I am doing. What I feel. You will send me away. You will lock the door. You will not invite me inside.'

'And what have you done?'

'I have fallen, Emma. Hard. And my body hurts from the impact. From the pressure on my chest. In my heart. Because it bleeds. With feelings. With love. My heart wants to love you. *I* want to love you,' he confessed, and he felt raw. Exposed. But he would not stop. He couldn't.

'I want to be on the inside, Emma. I want to be with you. I want to make this house our safe place. I want to come inside and be alone with you beside me. I want to bring all those things inside with us I have been trying to keep out. Emotion. Attachment. *Love*. Because I can no longer close the door on them. Because they live inside me. And they are stronger than the demons. They are in the process of exorcising them from me.'

A lightness spread over him, as he finally let it all out. Because he did. By God, he wanted all of those things. *Needed* them.

'I love you, Emma.'

And he waited for her to love him back.

'I have loved you since the moment I saw you. I have loved you every day since. You are where I come when I want to be still. When I want to close the doors and lock the world outside. It is *you* I come to. You are home to me. And without you, these last weeks, before your fall, I have been lost. I am homeless without you.'

He spread out the divorce papers on the ground before him. 'I came today to bring you the divorce papers,' he said, and his body revolted. It trembled with this choice. But he had made it this way.

He could be inside right now. But he was here on the pavement, waiting, as she had every time he went away, every time he left her behind and alone, waiting for him.

'I will sign them if that is what you want,' he said, and his voice was tight. 'If you want this, *us*, to end, I will do it. I will sign them. If you need more time to think, I will wait. I will wait for you forever.'

His chest heaved.

'You are my soulmate, Emma. Destiny thrust us together. And it will do it again. In this life, the next. I will wait for it. But I do not want the next life. I want *this* life. I want you to be my wife. A real wife with a real husband. I want to be your husband. I want everything I never thought I wanted because of you. Before you, I was empty. And you filled me up, Emma. With warmth. With love.'

Still, she did not move.

And it hurt. Deeply. The understanding that he might be too late. She might send him away because her needs no longer aligned with his.

'If you choose to sign,' he said, and his mouth moved in awkward ways. His tongue was too heavy. It did not want to cooperate. But he would keep his promise. 'If you choose to end us. I will keep my word. I will give you a divorce and I will…'

His jaw locked. His body hardened. But he would do it for her. He would sacrifice his needs to meet hers, because that was love.

And he loved her.

'I will let you go, Emmy.'

Her heart fluttered as wildly as a million bees buzzing towards home. Towards their queen. And it didn't matter to the bees where home was, because home was their queen.

Home was right in front of her.

Emma moved.

She let the bees carry her home. Until she stood in front of it. In front of him.

'I choose you,' she said. 'I choose our marriage.' She held out her hand. 'Because I love you.'

And she waited with bated breath for him to take her hand. To accept her love. To trust her to lead him to a safe place. Because it was safe. Their love protected them. And she would protect him now. She would shelter him. She would—

'Emmy…' His hand reached for hers. His fingers slid between hers. Entwining his between hers.

He stood. His face twisted with contorted angles of uninhibited emotion.

He pressed his forehead to hers. 'I love you. I love you with everything I am. Everything you have enabled me to become. I am changed because of you. And I—'

'You will let me in, you will let me love you and you will love me in return.'

'*Yes!* I will love you. With my words. With my body. With *everything*, Emmy,' he promised, and she knew he would keep his word. As he always had.

'Let's go inside,' she said, and she felt the tremble rip through him. The shudder.

He nodded. And Emma led him by the hand, up the white stone steps.

And together they closed the black door behind them. They shut out the hardness, the noise, and found home.

In each other.

EPILOGUE

Later that night...

THE BED WAS LARGE.

Dante stretched out his arms, his long legs, his feet—searching for her. The warmth of her tiny toes to stroke against his. Her soft body to pull into his. And he found her. He stroked his feet against hers, placed his hand on her hip and pulled her into the groove of his hips. Pushed his face into her hair and inhaled her.

His lungs were full.

He wasn't alone.

He wasn't cold.

He was warm.

He was loved.

'I need to tell you something,' she said, and rolled to face him. She reached for his face and cradled it. And she searched his eyes as he searched hers. 'Are you afraid?'

'No,' he said and reached for her face and held it as she held his. 'Are you?'

She shook her head. 'No.' The tip of her tongue

crept out to moisten the pink pout of her lips. 'But tomorrow we should call a doctor.'

'And what will we tell him?' He smiled. 'That we are in love?'

'Yes.' And she smiled, but it trembled. 'We should tell him against all odds—all improbability—we found each other. We found love. And because of that love, we have made a baby.'

'A baby?'

'I know it,' she husked. 'I know it, as I knew you would come back to me. Trusted it. Hoped when hope should have been dead. But it lived inside me.' She reached for his hand and placed his open palm on her naked stomach. 'As does our baby, Dante. It is growing inside me. And I'm not afraid. Because I know fate has given us both this gift. It is a miracle. Against all the odds. And we will keep our baby safe in whatever place we are. We will be the family we never had. We will have joy. We will have love.'

His finger moved over her stomach. The soft swell. 'Emma,' he growled as it swept over him. Warmth. The primal urge to shelter her with his body and protect her. Protect what was inside her. A child they had made. Because he believed her. Believed that the gods of old, of new, had answered his prayers.

'I love you, Emma,' he said because he did, because she was the gift he never expected.

She was his family.

'Kiss me, please,' she begged.

Dante kissed her, and she kissed him. With need. With longing for all the things they had and for all the things that were to come. And they gave themselves up to it.

To hope. To fate. To love.

* * * * *

Were you blown away by Italian Wife Wanted?
Then why not try these other passion-fuelled stories by Lela May Wight?

His Desert Bride by Demand
Bound by a Sicilian Secret
The King She Shouldn't Crave

Available now!